DEDICATION

"Loving you is all I need. Never take your love from me. I think I would lose my mind if you go away. Say you'll never leave my side, that forever you'll be mine. April Shower me with your love. Heaven must have smiled on me, like it did the earth that day. When God created the sun and said let there be light. I write your name across my heart and proclaim it to the stars above. April shower me with your love." April Showers- Dru Hill

Miracle Monet, you have been nothing but pure joy since I brought you home. Your mommy is a better person because of you, and I know that one day, you will make the world better. Having Autism doesn't make you different, it makes you unique. A lot of people don't

understand you and mistreat you because of it. That is their loss. If they even gave you a small chance, they would see how funny you are. There is not a day that goes by and you don't make me smile. You are my soul, my heartbeat, my world. You keep fighting against the odds and mommy will always have your back. I love you so much.

Johnnae Mariah, happy 18th birthday. I love you twin and I am proud of the woman you are becoming. My chocolate drop, forever.

Malik, my TT baby. Happy 21st birthday. You are officially grown, but you will always be my favorite. I love you and I'm glad I got to see you. No more deployments.

Ashunti, Happy 18th birthday auntie. I love you and you keep pushing to go forward. You have turned into someone I am proud to say is my baby. You keep pushing.

It seems like just yesterday, all of you were little kids. Laughing, and playing games. Look at you now. Take a look at all of our lives and strive to be better. We will support you every step of the way. I love you.

ACKNOWLEDGMENTS

MLPP, I am proud of all of us. We have come so far and if we keep pushing, we will break urban lit by storm. We have one of the greatest tools, Mz Lady P. Utilize her and continue to grow. She can't help us do anything if we aren't trying to listen. We got this. Keep coming strong.

Mz Lady P, thank you for all that you have done for me. I couldn't have asked for a better publisher. I'm also proud to be able to call you my friend. I love you.

ZaTasha, quit allowing people to discourage you. Bookies is a group you created in order to give authors a platform, and readers to find dope books. I appreciate everything you have done for every one of us. You're amazing and thank you for being a part of my life.

Krissy, I don't know how you just fought your way in. However you did it, I am grateful that you are here. Thank you for being there no matter the time or day. I can always count on you. I love you babes.

Lawrynn, my bestie. Thank you for allowing me into your world and your family. Honesty is rare now days, but you always keep it real with me. I appreciate you for not changing who you are. They keep trying to take my bestie, but I fight. Try me. I love you Kim and granny.

KB COLE, I never thought I could be so close to someone under another company, but you are my sister and I appreciate you so much. Your heart is big as gold and I am grateful to have crossed your path. Check out her books she is amazing.

Ashley, A.J Davidson. You are something else. You were supposed to give me a big head girl, but I will love our son just the same. LOL. You keep me laughing and I thank you for everything you do for me. Keep pushing, your season is coming. I love you. Check out her books she is so dope and I can't wait for Dope boys need love too. It's a best seller.

Panda, I love you girl Just keep pushing. Focus on the right things and everything else will fall into place. Check her out yall. She got dope books as well.

To my readers, I love you all so much and I could never explain how much I appreciate you. The Hoovers have been one of my biggest series, and it is all because of you. Blaze took your hearts by storm, and I'm glad that you all received him and loved his crazy ass. Keep rocking with me, and I will keep pushing to bring you some dope books. As I told you all, I will put some readers in each book of mine. If your name has not been said yet, don't worry, I have plenty books coming.

Lakeitha Chatman, you have been one of my biggest supporters from the start. Thank you for rocking with me. I love you girl and don't ever change.

Debra Watkins happy bday, Chandria Stanford, Huanna, Melissa Lampkins, Ivesha Harris, Janiece, Alesia Russel, Latoria, Rachel Pittman, Jasmine Rhoden, Joanne Mackins, Courtney Brownlee, Charlotte Bembry, Glenda Daniel, Rachel Hall, Narlonde, Tura Billingslea, Lashay Parson, Joan Brooks, Kat Dailey, Zatavia Robinson,

Ulyssesa Thomas, Tajuana Smith, Tahira Denae Smith, Danielle Guidry, Toy Smith, Mz Eve, Jasmine Williams.

I just want you to know that I appreciate you for being there for me. I love you.

SHADOW OF A GANGSTA

BY LATOYA NICOLE

ST. JOHN THE BAPTIST PARISH LIBRARY
2920 NEW HIGHWAY 51
LAPLACE, LOUISIANA 70068

WHERE WE LEFT OFF...

BLAZE...

We were finally back home, and I couldn't be happier. The shit was done, and my family made it out one last time on top. When paradise put the fire out, I was pissed. I wanted to see that bitch body turn to ashes. She turned to G and was smiling all goofy and shit.

"Hey G, you want to make a bet." When he started smiling back, me and my brothers looked at each other trying to figure out what the fuck was going on.

"This time, loser has to do everything dealing with Kenya bad ass for two months. Feeding, cleaning, babysitting the works."

"Bet."

"The fuck is you niggas talking about?" Suave pulled us out of the room laughing.

"You don't want to be in there for that. When they first met, they made a bet to see who could cut our parents up the smallest and fastest. Nastiest shit I ever seen. Let's go, let them have they moment."

"Nigga and you feeding a bitch to a dog wasn't nasty? All you niggas sick." We laughed as we waited outside for the nasty ass couple to finish. Them niggas was made for each other.

As much as we wanted they creepy ass to go back where the fuck they came from, watching them in the lobby with their bags didn't feel right.

"Shadow's birthday is tomorrow. Stay one more day and let us take yall out to thank yall."

"One more day nigga and we better have fun. I been dodging bullets and killing since I been here." Laughing at Suave, we all went upstairs to get ready. Out of everything we been through this month, I was more excited about this than anything. We hadn't been out in a year and I couldn't wait to party.

Throwing on my all black Gucci button up, black Gucci jeans, and my red high top Giuseppe's, I was ready to go. When we all made it down to the foyer, everybody looked like money. It was almost a billion dollars standing in this foyer and that right there was enough for me to be happy. Can't complain about the life we chose to live or the ups and downs that came with it. At the end of the day, we came out on top and lived to tell the story. Jumping in our Phantoms, G rode with me and Suave rode with Face.

As soon as we pulled up to Hoover Nights, I started smiling.

"Nigga, what the fuck you smiling at?"

"You have no idea. Watch this shit." When the first set of headlights went off the crowd went nuts. G looked at me all confused.

"What the fuck they screaming for?" Not responding, I just laughed and turned my lights off. Opening our door at the same time, we stepped out. G

and Suave stepped out as well and we walked to their side. The crowd was going crazy and people recognized who they were.

"Oh my God, Lucifer. Can I just touch your hand?" One of the girls screamed from the crowd.

"What kind of place is this?" Me and my brothers looked at each other and started doing our wave. The crowd joined in and started chanting.

"HOOVER. HOOVER. HOOVER." Suave was laughing, but G ass had to ruin our moment.

"Yall aggy as hell. If yall don't bring yall dumb ass on. I need a fucking drink and you out here waving and shit at the crowd like you the queen of England." Laughing, we all walked in the club. Of course, the crowd went nuts when they saw us.

"Awww shit, The Hoover Gang in the mother fucking building. Wait, did these niggas get Suave and Lucifer to come out and party with us. I need everybody to raise they fucking glasses and salute some real niggas. You in the presence of Legends." Everybody raised their cups as our song played.

"I think I'm Big Meech, Larry Hoover. Whipping work, hallelujah. One nation, under God real niggas getting money from the fucking start." BMF by Rick Ross played over the speakers as we partied with the crowd.

This was the life and I wouldn't apologize for nothing we had done. It made us who we are today and we some boss ass niggas with some bad bitches to hold us down. More money than we knew what to do with, how the fuck can you complain behind some shit like that? We had made it and we defeated all our enemies. Drea hadn't slipped on anymore dicks so life was great. We didn't have shit else to worry about and we could just live life how we wanted. Shadow came and stood by Gangsta and I didn't think shit of it until I heard him try to whisper.

"G, will you train me?"

CHAPTER ONE SHADOW

When I asked G to train me, the nigga looked at me and laughed. That was the problem, nobody took me seriously. That shit had to stop, I was ready to become that nigga. The city was going to fear me, and it would be because of my reputation, not my name.

"What the fuck you say purse dog?" Blaze was trying to lean in close as G questioned me, so I decided to leave it alone. There was no way I was going to allow my brothers to know what it was, until I was a fully trained hit man. Me and G would have our time to talk, and no one would be there to interfere.

Downing another drink, a nigga was feeling good and decided to enjoy the party with my brothers. Everybody was out there having a good time, but me. My ass was over here thinking about shit, and they ass was partying. Making my way to the crowd, I started dancing with my brothers to *Rake It Up by Yo Gotti.* I was all the way feeling myself until some nigga decided they wanted to try us.

"Look at these niggas. The Hoover Gang supposed to run the city, and they in here dancing like a bunch of bitches. Tough ass line dancers." This goofy ass nigga and his friends thought it was funny.

"Gone head on. We not on that shit tonight, so we gone let you make it. Let's be clear, I can change my mind quick, so move fast." You would think they would have taken Quicks warning, it's not often we give passes. G and Suave looked on to see how we would handle this. That was my cue to show him how I got down.

"The fuck yall gone do? Hit us with a milly rock and a dab." Before he could get his laugh out, the nigga went to sleep on his forehead. Not wasting any time, I two pieced his friend, and dropped another. All mayhem broke loose. We were stomping the niggas out.

When the bitch ass nigga finally woke up, he grabbed his gun and started shooting. Quick and G pulled their guns so quick, nobody knew they did until the other guys were hit. Our security finally found their way over to us and cleaned up the mess.

We were escorted out the back and waited for our cars to be brought around. This was why my brothers and them were ready to get out of the life. We never knew how the shit would go down, and we never knew if we would make it home at night.

"How the fuck them niggas keep getting guns in our shit? We the only niggas supposed to be carrying in that bitch." Blaze was pissed, and he was getting everybody else worked up.

"Yall security need they ass fired. They should have been there the minute purse dog laid the first nigga out. What kind of shit show operation yall running. Niggas wouldn't have fingers fucking with me." G wasn't making the shit no better.

"Fuck all that, the shit handled, and we get to go home to our families. You niggas get to go back to Hawaii, so all is well. I'm about to be out and go get some pussy, me and my girl got some making up to do." Baby Face was always the voice of reason, causing everybody to calm down.

"Fuck that, somebody getting they ass lit up tonight. I don't give a fuck who it is, I'm flicking this Bic. G, you riding with me? Bring your Harambe looking ass on. Me love bananas looking ass nigga." I know Blaze was bat shit crazy, because he wasn't scared to antagonize Gangsta. This nigga skinned people for a living.

"Naw, I'm gone ride with purse dog. I would have to beat your ass tonight, and I ain't in the mood for playing. I'll be done left you on Debra porch hanging. You too damn aggy for me. Extra ass nigga." This was my perfect opportunity, and I probably showed more enthusiasm than I meant to. Blaze flicked his Bic at G and walked off. As soon as my car pulled up, I jumped in ready to talk.

"Look lil nigga, I only rode with you to tell you no. This shit ain't for everybody. In another time, another life, you could have been my protégé. I'm retired, Paradise and Kenya mean more to me than being out there in them streets. You're twenty two, and you had a good run. Leave that shit where it's at." I would respect that, if I believed the bullshit he was spitting.

"I know you don't want to train me because you think I can't do it. Your ass ain't stopped killing since you retired, so don't give me that family bullshit. Answer this, if Blaze or Quick had opened the door and given you the same attitude, would you have treated them like you did me?" You could tell he thought about it long and hard before he answered.

"No, if it had been them, I would have killed them. Your brothers wouldn't have let me get the drop on them like that, and I would have known I had to take them out, or they would have taken me out. I get your point, but I still don't think you're ready.

You need to train with your brothers and them first. Hell, even Suave, you just don't jump out the door and train with a nigga like me. Baby steps nigga." Seeing that my stance wasn't gone change, he rubbed his hand down his face.

"Let me think on this shit, but if we do this, just know I'm not going to take it easy on you. By the time we are done, you are going to hate me. Your family is going to hate you, and you may lose your wife. I'll tell you again, this shit ain't for everybody. Make sure this is what you want. Now hurry the fuck up and drop me off. You niggas done stressed me the fuck out, and we were supposed to be partying." Laughing, I pulled up to the main house.

"Get the fuck out my shit and hit me up when you ready. Make sure you on your shit as well, rumor has it your old ass done got soft."

"Ain't shit soft on me but my balls bitch. Clown ass tried it. Now come open my fucking door, before I beat your ass." Not moving, he laughed as he got out. "You learning quick purse dog." His ass faded into the night, leaving me with my thoughts. This shit was about to get real fucking interesting, and I couldn't wait. He said he had to think on it, but I could see in his eyes the shit was a go. He had no idea how ready I was, I just wish I knew what it was going to be like.

****

"Purse dog, get your bitch ass up. I got something I need you to handle. Meet me outside on the back." I thought this nigga was supposed to be on the fucking plane by now. Looking at the clock, I groaned when I realized it was six in the morning.

Getting out of my bed, I headed downstairs. Not even bothering to wash my face or brush my teeth. This nigga couldn't want much, and I planned to get back in the bed as soon as we were done. It shocked me to see my brothers sitting in lawn chairs, and Paradise in a sports bra with leggings.

"What the fuck is going on G. I thought my brothers weren't supposed to know about this." I whispered to this nigga, as I pulled him to the side.

"They think we out here because you pissed me off in the car on the way home last night. I will train you on one condition." Not knowing what he had in mind, I waited for him to tell me. "You have to fight Paradise, and win." The nigga walked off leaving me looking stupid.

A nigga didn't fight women, I mean I knocked Sheree in her head about my ass, but that's as far as I've ever went. I was about to tell G I wasn't doing this shit, when Paradise hit me in my mouth. I think she shook my tooth loose.

"G, I don't know what kind of game yall playing, but get your girl." Punching me again, this time she busted my nose. I wasn't about to take much more of this. Before I could back out of the shit, the bitch kicked me.

"Shadow, I know you scared of G, but you gone stand there and let a chick beat your ass? Nigga fight back, pinch the bitch, trip her ass. Do something." Blaze was yelling from the sidelines while everybody laughed.

"Don't get fucked up bitch." Blaze flicked his Bic at G, and as soon as I started to laugh, Paradise hit me with a two piece. Enough was enough. This half breed ass bitch was about to get rocked. Catching her with a jab to the mouth, her ass didn't even blink. I was convinced Gangsta was around here beating her ass. Giving her a hit that would knock any nigga out, I got pissed when she barely budged. Ready to get this shit over with, I charged her, but she saw the shit coming a mile away. She caught my ass mid run by my throat, and body slammed my ass. I could see the disappointment in G's face, and I knew he wasn't gone train me. I got my ass beat by a woman. When she climbed on top of me, her ass wouldn't stop punching my ass. The last hit gave me an idea. Pulling her to me, I blew my breath in her face. Paradise jumped up quick as hell. Paradise took off so fast, she damn near fell in the pool.

"That nigga won. Fuck that. Who would do something like that in a fight. Nigga breath smell like last day of period. Fuck he eat last night? Nasty bitch." Everybody laughed, and I just shrugged my shoulders.

Any means necessary. That's the type of niggas me and my brothers were. Our ass was gone win at any cost. We weren't taking no L's. Limping upstairs, I got my ass back in the bed. It felt like I got hit by a damn truck.

CHAPTER TWO GANGSTA

Packing up our stuff, I got the idea for Shadow and Paradise to fight. If that nigga couldn't handle her, there was no point in us even entertaining the thought of me training him. This shit was gone be done right, or not at all.

"Baby do you really think he ready for this shit? You know this shit ain't for everybody. It's a reason his brothers kept him from this shit." Paradise didn't really care for purse dog, but that wasn't the reason she didn't want me to train him.

"You do know I'm not getting back in the game right? You don't have to worry about that. I'm training him to be his own person, and that's it." You could tell she didn't believe my ass. A nigga breathed that shit, and no matter how many times we said we were done, our ass always seemed to be dragged back in.

"You say that shit now. How the fuck I even get in this shit? Got my ass about to fight and shit, when I'm trying to get ready for my fucking flight. You keeping Kenya ass for a month if I do this shit." Now her ass was playing dirty, and I wasn't going no matter what the fuck she said.

"How I'm gone get the baby if I'm gone be training? You wanted her bad ass, you got her. Now bring your ass downstairs and whoop this nigga so my dick can get hard. I need some pussy before we go." We laughed and headed downstairs.

After the fight, I knew he had it in him, but the shit was gone take a lot of work. This nigga barely won, and it wasn't because of his hands. My girl was rocking that nigga, until he blew his breath on her. I ain't gone lie, that shit was funny as hell. A nigga didn't want to admit it, but I was gone miss these niggas.

"Yall better come to Hawaii to check on a nigga. We gotta do this shit soon." Everybody was eerily quiet, like they were thinking the same thing.

"This shit was fun as fuck." We all turned to look at Blaze like he was crazy. How in the fuck was it fun when we were constantly fighting for our damn life?

"You got issues mother fucker." Quick was shaking his head at his brother.

"You got bald spots nigga if you keep fucking with me." When the nigga flicked his Bic, I knew it was time for me to get the fuck on. This nigga was trigger happy with a damn lighter. Paradise ear was still fucked up.

"Aight yall, we out. See you niggas soon." Everybody said their goodbyes and we were gone. The ride to the airport was quiet as hell. I couldn't help but wonder if Suave was gone miss this shit too. The thrill of it all had a nigga feeling young again.

"You can get that shit out of your head bitch. Try me if you want to I'll beat your ass out here." I couldn't do shit but laugh, it's like Paradise was reading my mind.

"Call me another bitch, I promise imma lay your ass out, and tie your ass to the back of the plane. Gone be a dangling hoe for eight hours. Your ear barely made it back on this mother fucker. Tell the truth, it was you that burned Blaze mustache and eyebrows off wasn't it?" When she laughed, I shook my head. Her and Blaze played too much for me. I be ready to peel a nigga neck off, and they ass around here doing goofy shit.

"You know damn well I wasn't gone let that nigga get one up on me. He can't even retaliate because he done fucked over everybody. Nigga don't know who to flick at." She was right, but I wasn't gone let her have that shit.

"Yea, but if you piss me off, I'm telling. Your ass better walk on that straight line from here on out. I'll drop a dime on your ass so quick, you won't know what hit your ass until that fire got ya." I was laughing, but she knew I was dead ass serious.

"You a snitch bitch."

"Just call me snitch bitch G."

"Thelma and Louise, can yall shut the fuck up. Damn, a nigga need some rest. Tank which one of these bitches you think is Thelma?" Suave ass was always trying to throw slugs.

"Thelma was the ugly one, so I'm rolling with G."

"Fuck yall." As we got settled on the plane, I laid down to try and clear my head. It was a lot on my plate. I had to train this nigga without getting sucked back in and making sure he didn't get hurt. I didn't like the idea of another nigga being my responsibility, but purse dog had grown on me. This shit was gone have to go smooth, or my ass would be going up against The Hoover Gang. Even though I was deadlier, them bitches was aggy as fuck. There is no doubt in my mind, I would have to kill Blaze first. Nigga play too much. Mother fuckers like me don't play. I'm all about death and money. If the shit ain't about that, it doesn't make sense.

****

Before we actually started the real training, I needed to make sure Shadow could get out of fucked up situations if need be. I was about to take him through a pre-training course. If his ass couldn't get through this shit, I was walking away. His brothers each possessed a skill, purse dog didn't have any that I could see. We needed to figure out what the lil nigga was good at other than fighting.

"Where the fuck your Kimbo Slice looking ass going? I didn't think you would start training this damn soon. We only been home a week."

"Shut the fuck up and get ready. We have to pick up Shadow for the G training. Let's see if this lil nigga got it in him."

"You know he don't. Only thing his black ass good for is hiding in the dark. Got me up this early wasting my damn time. Move. Dumb ass ain't even washed your face. Nut all in your beard." Not about to play with her ass this early, I pushed her making her fall down the stairs. Running in the bathroom, I got ready. First thing I did was wash my face. Nigga too fly to be walking around with left over pussy on his face.

Making sure we were good, we grabbed our bags and headed back to the airport. This was gone be the hardest part of training. All the back and forth was gone irritate the fuck out of me. Thank God we had our own plane. Getting settled on the plane, we headed back to Chicago.

Once we got off, we headed straight to the warehouse. Normally, we would have left Kenya with Tank and Suave, but we needed her for the first test.

Me and Paradise set up the interrogation room, and I grabbed what I needed and headed out. Driving over to Shadow house, I wondered how he would react.

CHAPTER 3 SHADOW

A nigga was sleeping good as hell until I felt somebody cover my face. Panic set in, and I had no idea if they already got to Kimmie. The way they were holding my head, it stopped me from being able to look. My ass tried to swing at whoever it was, but my body was weak. Not being able to fight it, I passed out.

When I opened my eyes, I had no idea where I was. I knew I was in some kind of warehouse, but I didn't know who had me. Trying to think clear, and get myself out of the situation, I looked around for something that could help me. Not seeing anything, I was pissed at myself. With all the beef we overcame, we should have been moved out of our old houses. All of our enemies knew exactly where to find our ass, and that has become a problem. Now my dumb ass here not knowing if my wife and baby are okay. It took me too long to get her pregnant, if these fuck niggas made her lose the baby, The Hoovers were coming back with a vengeance.

"Where do you and your brothers keep the money?" A distorted voice came through a speaker, and I couldn't make out who it was. It was as if they were using a device to change their shit, which told me it may be somebody we knew.

"What money?" I decided to see how much they would say.

"You have five minutes to tell me where the money is, or we gone have a problem. Every minute after the five I give you, one of your brothers will die. In eight minutes, your entire world gone shift. It's up to you how the shit plays out." Knowing I had to figure out a way to warn my brothers, I tried to break free. Whoever tied me to this chair had to be a professional. Struggling to get away the entire five minutes, I heard the speaker and knew my time was up.

"Where the fuck is the money?"

"I'll take you to it, but you have to untie me first." It got quiet, and by the time I realized someone was behind me, they had already covered my head, and tied it closed. I don't know what the nigga hit me with, but my ass did the Milly Rock in that bitch. His ass might have knocked the answer out of me, and I didn't even know it. After a few more minutes, I was at the top of the steps about to enter that upper room. At least that's what it felt like, when he finally stopped. The speaker came back on.

"You already lost Baby Face, and you done got your ass handed to you on a platter. Tell me where the money is before you lose any more."

"I can take you to mine. Them niggas don't tell nobody where they shit at. All I can give you is mine. I have about twenty mil saved up. That should be enough."

"Did I ask you for twenty mil, or did I ask for it all?" When I didn't respond, I knew it was about to get ugly.

"Wrong choice." The nigga hit me again, and his ass had to hit me with a hammer or something. Ain't no way that nigga hit me so hard, my ass started beat boxing. It almost felt as if I shitted on myself. Now I see how it feels when I be rocking a nigga. Realizing I had taken a quick nap, I tried to plead my case.

"Look, don't be greedy. Just take mine, and we will call it even." The speaker came back on, and I knew I had just lost another brother.

"Quick kind of slow for a nigga that's supposed to be fast. He didn't suffer though. Now Blaze, I can't promise you how that is going to go." Tears fell down my face, and it wasn't because of the pain. I was frustrated it was nothing I could do to save my brothers. This was not how this shit was supposed to go. Another tear fell, but that bitch was knocked through my mask. This nigga had some haymakers, and I wished he would gone and end my ass. My brothers were gone anyway, and it was all of us, or none of us. There was no way I could live with myself, and they all were gone. The assault went on for a little while longer, and the tears came again because I knew what he was about to tell me. Blaze was aggy as fuck, but that was my nigga. I loved all my brothers, but Blaze held a special place in all of our hearts. It will never be another Blaze.

"I'm sure you already know what I'm about to tell you, but what you don't know is how he died. Blaze was drenched in gasoline and burned until it was nothing left of that nigga. Now maybe you don't love your brothers like I thought you did, but what about your pregnant wife? Would you tell me where the money is, if I cut your baby out of her stomach and bring it to you? What if I set the baby on fire right in front of you? Would you talk then?" As much as this shit hurt, there was no way I could give in to this nigga. Most people would say I was dumb, and it ain't shit but money. I'm just not cut from that cloth. None of us are. What pissed me off the most was the fact that they chose to question me. That tells me they thought I was the weak link. Fuck them, and everything they stood for. Knowing he was coming back in here to beat my ass, I tried to prepare myself for it.

The hit never came, but I felt something dropping on me. I couldn't figure out what it was at first, until the smell hit me. What the fuck? Somebody was shitting on me, and it smelled like dead goat ass. Feeling them try to untie me, I knew they were about to attempt to shit in my mouth, or on my face. A nigga went crazy trying to get away. I saw Blaze do that shit to Kimmie, and that was some nasty shit. Flipping back in my chair, I was now in the perfect position for them to do it. Trying my best to roll over, I damn near broke my leg until I heard laughing. I had no idea what the fuck was going on. The bag came off my head, and I was looking at Gangsta, Paradise, and nasty ass Kenya.

"Are you fucking kidding me? What kind of sick ass game are you playing? You think this shit funny?"

"Naw, but it's funky than a mother fucker. You did all that to get away from the shit, and your ass landed right in it. Good job baby girl. Daddy gone take you to get some ice cream okay. Untie that shitty ass nigga so he can go back home. Congratulations purse dog, you just passed G training part one. Be ready nigga, you never know when I'm coming. Keep that shit in mind while you at home laid up all cozy and shit. This what you wanted, well nigga you got it."

"Nigga you damn near broke my jaw and shit. What kind of training is this?"

"If a nigga grabs you, I needed to make sure nothing could break you. I'm a different kind of nigga Shadow. I've done a lot of shit in my life, and a lot of mother fuckers out here hate my guts. I can't surround myself with a weak nigga. I trust your brothers with my life, if I'm going to train you, I need to feel the same about you. Get the fuck out of your feelings and be proud. You passed test one. Pass the rest, and you will have officially earned my respect. You keep bitching, training starts over. We don't do weakness of any kind.

Remember that shit. Now go the fuck home and clean up. Be ready and find a good lie to tell your people. Nobody is to know you're training with me."

I was pissed, but the shit made sense. Paradise untied me, and I swear I wanted to drop kick Kenya's ass to the moon.

"How am I supposed to get home?" The nigga shrugged his shoulders and left my ass there looking stupid.

CHAPTER 4 GANGSTA

I ain't gone lie, purse dog surprised the shit out of me. He not built like his brothers, and I didn't think he could take torture like that. I'm really starting to like this nigga. There aren't many people that can take the kind of test I put him through, but I'm not done. By the time I'm through testing him, nobody will ever be able to question his loyalty. If he completes it.

"Baby Hoover got some heart. You were rocking his ass, and he still stood his ground. I'm shocked." Paradise felt the same way I did, and that shit made me smile. I hope he completed the rest of it, and then I could feel like a proud father.

Me and Paradise were finally home, but I needed to go talk to Suave. Even though Shadow couldn't tell his people, I needed to talk this shit over with my brother. He would tell me if I needed to back off this shit. Suave could read a nigga with his eyes closed. Knocking on the door, I didn't get an answer. Needing to talk to him, I used my key and walked in.

Since my ass didn't get no pussy last night, I stood there and watched their nasty ass. Suave was eating Tank's ass like a full course meal. Who would have ever thought shit could taste so good. His nasty ass was moaning and shit like it was him getting his shit ate. Why they were in the front room having a full sex session was beyond me, but I was ready to go home and give Paradise the business. I got so caught up in their shit, I forgot I shouldn't be in there. My ass started giving advice and shit.

"Slide two fingers in her and stroke her clit." They both jumped up and looked at me like I was crazy.

"G, your ass a pervert. Get the fuck out of my house before I beat your ass."

"Nigga I need to talk to you, can you climb out the pussy for a second?" Seeing that I was serious, he came to talk.

"Tank go to the room and keep that shit wet for me, I'll be there in a minute." The nigga actually came and sat down in my face.

"Mother fucker if you don't go brush your teeth first. You were just tonsils deep in her asshole. You probably got shit chips in your throat. If your ass cough and the shit fly on me, I swear I'm shooting you bitch." Laughing, he got up to go handle his hygiene. When it took him forty five minutes to come back from brushing his teeth, I knew his bitch ass got some pussy first.

"Aight, what you want to talk about? I held her off for a little while, but when that clit starts jumping, she ain't gone wait that long." Getting right to the point, I told him my dilemma since we didn't have much time.

"Shadow wants me to train him, and I kind of told him yea."

"That's why you had Paradise fighting him. You do realize your bitch crazy, but she can get that ass spanked. I wish you would ever send her my way, imma lay her ass out like Quick's edges."

“Nigga can you stay on track. Do you think he has it in him? We know how his brothers get down, but he didn’t grow up like us.”

“It’s only because he was younger. Don’t underestimate him. That nigga didn’t blink when you had him bash Royalty head off. Smalls been around us for years, and you never seen him join in on the shit we do. That should tell you a lot.”

“I get that bro, but I’m a different kind of nigga. You know me. I have a sick side to me, and I don’t want to pull that nigga into my lifestyle. This shit ain’t for everybody. You have to already have that shit inside of you.”

“What are you really scared of G? When have you ever cared about another nigga’s life? If you bring him into your world and he can't take it, so be it. He didn't lose out on shit. Nigga might lose his breakfast, but nothing that he can't shake off." Thinking about his question, I answered as honest as I could.

"If the shit goes bad, I have to explain the shit to his brothers. I'm not sure I could face them. These are our brothers. They respect me and look up to a nigga. Now I'm going behind their back doing some shit I know they wouldn't approve of." You could see that he was thinking hard on what I was saying.

"You are the only nigga I trust one hundred percent to have my back. You won't let nothing happen to him. I'm sure of it. Now get your head in the game. Whether you train him or not, he will find someone else to do it because he not happy with his shit. Why not be trained by the best. You got this baby bro. If you didn't, I would advise you to leave him where he at."

"Aight, now he just has to pass the last two tests. If he does, then we go into official training. If he doesn't, I'm gone beat his ass for wasting my time and fuck his bitch."

"Bye nigga, I got some pussy to get in to." Dapping him up, I headed out the door. I felt better about the shit. If Suave agreed with it, then I knew I wasn't making a mistake. Walking in my door, I was ready to get this shit going to see what purse dog was made of. Feeling something whip me across my back, I instantly drew my gun.

Paradise was standing behind me in some leather shit, carrying a whip. She must have lost all of her mind.

If I wasn't a calculated shooter, her ass would have a bullet between her eyes, and that shit ain't sexy at all.

"What the fuck are you doing? I just almost shot your super hero looking ass. Why you in here looking like an extra from Cat woman and shit?" Her petty ass hit me again. I'm not with that freaky white shit and I was ready to beat her ass.

"Damn G, let's do something different. I read this sex scene in this book called *A Mayhem Love by Bianca*, he was turned on when she was beating his ass. Let me just try it and see if you like it." She had me fifty shades of fucked up. Her and this Bianca chick.

"Hit me with that shit again, and your ass gone be a couch in somebody grandma house. In here looking dumb as hell in all that hot ass leather. We are in Hawaii, how the fuck was I supposed to peel that shit off?"

"Fuck you. Can't even do no sexy shit for your ass. All you want to do is fuck. Uh uh uh. Turn over Uh uh uh." Trying not to laugh, I pulled her to me. Her ass was burning up in that hot ass shit.

"You want to try something different? Get on your knees." She rolled her eyes but got down anyway. Pulling my dick out, I slapped her in the face with my shit to get it hard. Pushing her mouth on my dick, you could tell she thought she was gone take the lead. Forcing my shit all the way to the back, I didn't give her time to catch her breath. Grabbing her by her neck, I fucked her mouth while I choked her. My bitch wanted rough, she was about to get all this dick today. I ain't have shit but time, and I needed something rough. This was what I loved most about Paradise. She never complained about rough sex, she loved that shit.

Her moans were driving me crazy, and I was trying not to nut. The shit didn't work for long, and in seconds I was releasing down her throat. When I released her neck, she looked like she was on the verge of passing out.

"Oh, you eating this ass tonight. Bitch you got me fucked up." Dragging her to the room, I laughed. Everybody was on this ass eating shit tonight. Hey, like I said before, I got time today.

CHAPTER 5 SHADOW

"Where the fuck are you going now? You came in the other night beat the fuck up at five in the morning. What bitch you fucking and her nigga caught you?" I've been hearing this shit since G decided he wanted to be on some sneak kidnapping shit.

"I already told you, some niggas jumped me, and I passed out. Do you think I want to hear this shit? I'm out here trying to figure out who the fuck did this shit to me. I don't have time to be in the house arguing with your insecure ass." Kimmie was really starting to piss me off, but I knew if I told her what I was really doing, she would kill me.

"You got me fucked up. Let me find out who the bitch is, I promise you and that hoe dead. Nigga known for cheating, but I'm insecure. Fuck out of here. If I'm insecure, you made me that way." Knowing I couldn't stay in here arguing, I had to end the shit.

"I ain't make you shit. I'm telling your ass ain't no other bitch. Now if you choose not to believe that, then it's on you. I was with my ex for years, and I never married her ass. I knew your ass less than a year, but you a fucking Hoover. For once, act like it." Grabbing my keys, I walked out the door.

If I told her what was really going on, I know it would ease her mind. She would know I'm not cheating on her, but it would make shit a lot worse. I promised her that I was retired, yet here I was. She wasn't the only one I would have to deal with, my brothers would be on good bullshit. They would talk G out of the shit, but I needed this for me. No one would understand that. G wanted to see if I could handle business without him. He was mainly out of the game and wouldn't be able to do runs as much.

My test tonight was to see how I would handle myself in a run without no one there to protect me. Usually it's me and my brothers. I've never done shit like this by myself. Gangsta said if I couldn't do something as simple as this, then it was no point in training me. Now me and my brothers never did drug runs, but I wanted to prove to G I could do this.

Going to the address he gave me, I picked up ten kilos of drugs. I thought I would be nervous about the shit, but I wasn't. Adrenaline was running through me, and a nigga was excited as hell to be doing this shit all on my own. Pulling up the warehouse, I grabbed my gun. Making sure it was loaded, I got out of the car and grabbed the bag. This should be a smooth transition since they already knew I was coming. However, I still took precautions.

Walking in the building, the guy and his security was already inside waiting on me. Security checked me as I thought they would and took my gun. I never understood that shit though. Was there someone in here that searched them, and took their shit? Who the hell decides which guys decides to keep their guns?

Sitting down, I held on to my bag. I needed to make sure everything was cool before I handed anything over.

"Where is Gangsta? I thought he was coming to the meeting?"

"He couldn't make it, but I'm here and we can move forward with the transaction."

"You can give us the drugs now and get up out of here. Hand it over, and you get to walk out of here with your life." This nigga thought it was sweet.

"Don't play with me my nigga. Give me the money, and I'll be the fuck up out of here." They all raised their guns, and I knew it wasn't going to be an easy night. I was so sick of niggas trying me when I wasn't with my brothers, I allowed the anger to take over me.

Reaching inside my bag, I slid my extra gun out of the side pocket. There was no way I was going out like Willie Lump Lump. I really needed to figure out who the fuck that was. Everybody always said that, but nobody knew who the fuck was Willie. Before I could even raise my gun, the shots hit me in my chest. Falling out of the chair, the wind was knocked out of my ass. Trying hard to breathe, I couldn't believe I fucked this up. Laughter was the last thing I heard before everything went black.

Looking around, my mind was racing. The jokes, laughs, and shit talking about me like I was a lil nigga started to get to me. My brothers and his friends always thought I was the weak link. Everybody thought I was the soft one, and I was sick of that shit. The only thing my mind told me was to get the fuck up and start shooting. That's exactly what the fuck I did. Hitting the first nigga, I grabbed the bag and kept right on shooting. Not looking back, I blasted my gun until I made it outside. Once I was in my car safe, I saw guys running behind me and I got the fuck up out of there.

Driving as fast as I could, I got the fuck away from that warehouse. It was a good thing I decided to wear my vest, or my ass would be dead. The shit still hurt like hell, but I was alive. Reaching in my pocket, I grabbed my phone. There was no way that shit would have went down if G was there. His ass was gone have to get on a flight tonight. I wanted those niggas to be my first target. They had me fucked up. Before I could even hit send, I heard the sirens behind me. Fuck. My night was already messed up, but it was about to get worse.

Pushing the bag of drugs to the floor, I pulled over and tried to remain calm. All I had to do was talk normal, and not look like I was on some shit. Everything would be cool. Letting my window down, I waited for the officer to approach my window.

"This is a nice car you got here. Not too many out here, especially this time of night." Wishing now I hadn't drove my Phantom, I nodded and gave a fake smile. "It's funny, we just got a call about a shoot out and the guy running and jumping in an all black Phantom." Knowing this shit wasn't about to go as smooth as I thought, I reached for my wallet in an attempt to smooth things over.

“Here is my license and registration. What is my ticket for?” The bitch ass nigga actually laughed.

“Ticket? You fit the description of a man that was just in a shoot out, you were doing almost a hundred when I pulled you over, and you’re sweating like crazy. The first thing I’m going to do is search your car. Do you have anything in here I should know about?” Shaking my head, I stepped out of the car. There was no way I was telling on myself. He was gone do his own fucking job. Cuffing me, he sat me on the curb, while he looked through my shit.

As soon as he opened my door, he found the bag of drugs. Searching the rest of the car, he came up with nothing. Getting out, he picked me up and searched me. Grabbing the gun, I knew it was over for a nigga like me.

Even though my lawyer could get me out on bail, I knew there was no way the judge was giving me anything less than ten years.

"You know you fucked up right? Your ass is going down for a long time. Get the fuck in the car. I can't wait for them to auction this bitch, maybe I'll buy it for myself." Laughing, I knew there was no way his bitch ass would be able to buy a car like this. I would have to tell my brothers what the fuck was going on now, cus I needed them to get me out of here.

The bitch ass officer laughed damn near the entire way to the station talking shit. Driving in the back, I hoped he wasn't about to beat my ass, but he took me in a back door and led me to a room. My ass was sweating bullets as I waited for him to come back. After about thirty minutes, he finally walked back in with a folder.

"Zavien Hoover, so we finally meet. We been after you and your brothers for a long time. Now we have your ass thanks to the gun we caught on you. How cocky can you be to keep the same damn gun after all the shit you have done?"

"Can I call my lawyer?"

"When I'm done, you sure are going to need him. For now, I'm trying to make a deal with you."

"I'm not giving up my brothers, so you may as well do what you need to do. Let me get my call and press your charges." His bitch ass got me fucked up.

"I don't want your brothers. They are going down without your help. Trust me, we don't need you for them. We want the untouchable. Gangsta and Suave."

This nigga had lost his damn mind.

"If you know who they are, why the fuck would I turn against them? Get me my phone call, and I promise to buy your big ass some food when I get out of here. You sounding real hungry right now, bitch ass barely making it."

"Look, we can protect you. We will give you and your brothers immunity if you just give us those two. Do you know how much time you're facing?" I didn't give a fuck if they were giving me the chair. Nobody in their right mind would turn on G and Suave. I still wasn't convinced those niggas didn't eat people. G looked like he done had an elbow or two in his lifetime.

"I don't give a fuck what you are offering. Get me my phone call, I don't have shit to say to you. Just to be nice, I will still buy you a meal." When he walked out of the room, another nigga walked in. This was a game I would never get tired of playing. There was no way I would snitch on a nigga that eat thighs and shit.

"Do you know the type of charges we have on you and your brothers? I don't think you understand the kind of time you're facing. Your brothers will never see daylight again. We may get a chance at the death penalty. Yet you are sitting here cocky and shit like you have a choice in the matter." What the fuck kind of luck did I have today. Only I would get myself caught in this kind of shit. G was going to be so disappointed in me. I fucked all this shit up.

"Do what you have to do with me. Whatever charges you have on my brothers, I'll confess to it."

"Do you know what you are saying?" Knowing my life was over, I nodded my head. There was no way I would allow my brothers to go down for my mistakes. It was absolutely no way I would turn on G and Suave.

"Yea, I know. Give me a pen and I'll sign everything." They both got up and walked out of the room. Laying my head on my desk, I can't believe I'll never get to be a father to my kid. My family, all that shit is gone. All because I was insecure in a fucking reputation. FUCK. When I heard the door open, I knew my life was over and it wasn't shit I could do about it.

"Good job purse dog." When I heard his voice, my head snapped up. "We will start training soon. Go home and get some rest, you did good. Your car is outside."

"How the fuck were you behind this? This is a fucking police station." The nigga started laughing at me, but I didn't find the shit funny at all.

"Nigga my brother was the biggest king pin Chicago had ever seen. You really think we didn't have police in our pocket. You loyal as fuck, but you dumb as hell. Just in case you haven't put the shit together, the warehouse was all me as well."

"Nigga I had to shoot my way out that bitch. What if I killed them? I know I hit one of them."

"Well, everyone knows you can't shoot. I was banking on that, and they were heavily protected.

Shooting is definitely going to be part of your training, but you did hit one though. All of their asses have been taken care of. Go home and get some sleep."

This shit was unbelievable, jumping up, all I wanted to do was get the fuck home. This shit may have been a mistake. This nigga was testing me in another kind of way. His ass played too many sick games. For some reason, the thought of that excited me.

CHAPTER 6 GANGSTA

Looking at the camera in the warehouse, a nigga started to panic when Shadow went down. I didn't quite think the plan through. In my mind, I rationalized it by saying if he is smart he will wear a vest. A nigga didn't really know if he was actually that smart. His ass was out for about twenty minutes, and I didn't know what to do.

For the first time in a long time, a nigga was scared as shit. I was gone have to kill his brothers if this nigga didn't make it. Finally coming to grips that I needed to do something, I walked out to see if he was really dead. Mad at myself, I was dreading having to make this call. Right as I approached the niggas I had to set him up, Shadow got up shooting.

The lil nigga had me proud until he hit one of my men. The shit was supposed to be simple, but it just got complicated. Shadow didn't see one of my men coming on the side of him about to blow his brains out, and I couldn't allow that to happen. Irritated that I was about to lose my entire crew, I grabbed my gun and laid all of them down in five seconds flat. The only men standing were the niggas that were securing the outside of the building.

Shadow never looked back, so he never the guys on the inside were dead. Thinking of another plan, I walked outside and killed the men that was chasing Shadow's car down. Grabbing my phone, I called one of the officers on our payroll.

"Hey nigga, I need a favor. A very expensive favor." His ass got quiet, and I could hear a door close.

"How expensive?"

"I need you to arrest Shadow Hoover. Interrogate him and make him think you got some shit on him. I need to know will he turn on me if I work with him. I'm testing his loyalty. Do you think you can handle that? It's a twenty thousand dollar favor."

"Say no more. Where can I find him?" After giving him the last location Shadow was heading, I made my way to the station. I needed to see it in action. You can look a nigga in his eyes and see fear. Even if he doesn't break I needed to know how he handled these kind of situations.

Shocked wasn't even the word when I heard that nigga say he will sign a confession to all of the murders. I hoped he wouldn't talk, but I never thought he would cop to all the shit. Even I wasn't doing that shit. My ass would have shot my way up out that bitch, and worried about the shit later.

This nigga done got his ass whooped, shitted on, set up, shot, and arrested and not once did he even think about breaking. This nigga might be stronger than all of us. In that moment, I knew exactly how I was going to train him. I was gone teach him everyone's craft. This lil nigga had me all in my feelings smiling and shit.

Driving back to the airport, I couldn't wait to get home. I hate when shit almost go bad, it always takes me back to the time I thought I lost Suave and Paradise.

Needing to be around my girl, I hoped the flight was quick and smooth.

Waking up, I realized the plane had landed and my ass was home. Tired was not even the word, and I couldn't wait to get my ass in the bed. The drive home was quick, and I damn near ran in the house. It was quiet as hell, and in my line of business, that's not a good thing. My daughter was bad as hell, why the hell wasn't her ass woke and shitting every damn where?

Pulling my gun out, I walked quietly through my house. Checking in Kenya's room, she was sound asleep. Walking towards my room, I eased the door open. Paradise was in the middle of our room spinning on a pole. When I say her ass was spinning, I had to look hard to make sure it was her. If it wasn't for her body, I would have thought it was somebody else. The dim lights, and flickering candles had the shit looking sexy as fuck. Dropping my bags, I came out of my pants fast as hell and walked over to the pole. Pushing me down in a chair, she made me sit back and watch the show.

"Personal dances are twenty dollars. If you want to go to the VIP room, it's five hundred dollars. No touching, just sit back and enjoy the show." My girl had my dick brick hard and talking was the last thing on my mind. Paradise was fine as hell and perfect in almost every way, but my baby couldn't dance. She had to have taken lessons.

Her ass was twirling around that pole like a real stripper, and those high ass shoes she had on should have made the shit hard. When my baby dropped down in a split, it was over for me. Getting up, I tried to walk up on her, but she stopped me.

"Don't make me call security." Knowing she didn't really have any, I continued to approach her. "Biggs, we have a customer that won't comply." My ass was laughing hard at her role playing, until some big burly ass nigga stepped into the room.

"Sir, I'm going to need you to step away from Lips. We have a no touch rule." Looking at this nigga like he was crazy, I was about to beat his ass.

"If you don't get your Fair east side looking ass out my face. Hairline looking like, they used to call me crazy Joe, but now they call me batman. Mother fucking hair disabled than a mother fucker. Bitch ass." Paradise was laughing, but the nigga didn't find it funny, and tried to run up. Not even hesitating, I pulled the trigger and shot him between the eyes. Not even blinking twice, I walked over to Paradise. Dropping down in another split, she took my dick in her mouth. I don't know if it was just the idea of the split, but this was the best head I ever had in my life.

When she got to my balls, she would go up and down in her split, and the shit was driving me crazy. Pulling her up by her hair, I pushed her over as she held on to the pole for grip.

"You better fuck me good and hard or get your ass from back there." Smacking her as hard as I could on her ass, I wanted her to shut up. I've always given her this long dick, why the fuck would I stop now.

"Shut the fuck up." Pushing my dick inside of her, she gripped my shit with her muscles. "That's right baby fuck this dick. Throw that shit back." Her pussy started gushing, and a nigga was trying his best to control his nut. The moment I felt her gushing all over my meat, I let that shit ride. I couldn't hold it a second longer.

"Now pay me my money nigga. That will be five hundred dollars." Reaching in my wallet, I grabbed my credit card. "What the fuck are you doing?"

"You know I don't carry cash, now bend that ass over and let me tip drill you." Laughing, she bent over, and I swiped the card through her ass cheeks. Grabbing my phone, I dialed my brother.

"Hey, I need a clean up crew at my house. As soon as possible. If Kenya wakes up she will be in here trying to shit all over the nigga."

"What the fuck. Aight, let me call them." Hanging up the phone, I headed to the shower to wash all of today's events off. As soon as I stepped out of the shower, Suave and the clean up crew was there.

"Nigga what the fuck did you do? What happened?" You can tell Suave was pissed. We didn't want our old life to show up here in Hawaii.

"Ask your dumb ass sister in law. She thought it would be funny to hire security while she pretended to be a dry ass stripper."

"Don't try it bitch, your ass was begging me to hit that pole one more time. I just figured it would go with the role playing." Paradise actually tried to justify that shit.

"You do know who your husband is? Why the fuck would you think that shit was okay? Something wrong with you mother fuckers. How did the loyalty training go?" I knew I was gone have to tell Suave sooner or later.

"The nigga actually did extremely well. Shocked the shit out of me. We had some mishaps along the way." He looked at me with that I knew you was gone fuck up look. "I kind of didn't think it through all the way, and the entire crew is dead." The nigga stood over me like he was about to knock my ass out.

"Explain to me how something like that happens, and what do you mean by the entire crew?"

"I sent the nigga on a run that was a set up. The crew knew about it, but Shadow didn't. I assumed he would be wearing a vest, and they shot him. Good news is, he was wearing one. Bad news is, he woke up blasting. The crew didn't take kindly to that and started shooting back. One of them was about to fade his ass, and I kind of intervened."

"By intervening, you mean you shot everybody?" Nodding my head, the nigga actually laughed. He so uptight sometimes, I just knew we were gone have to square up. "As long as Smalls is good, I don't give a fuck. They knew the plan, they should have pretended to shoot back. Not actually try to take his ass out. That's on them lil niggas. I'll call Smalls and let him know he gotta recruit."

"Your ass better had understood. I thought I was gone have to whoop your ass." Before I got the last word out, the nigga slammed the shit out my ass. He won the fight, but before my back completely hit the ground, my gun was on that nigga."

"Nigga please." Looking over, he had his gun pointed at my head. I keep telling your ass, I'm not that old and I taught your bitch ass." Dapping up, he laughed and walked out. Now that I knew it was good with my brother, I could climb back in my pussy.

CHAPTER 7 SHADOW

I hadn't heard from G in a few days, and I was happy as hell. A nigga needed time to recuperate, and with the type of shit he was on, I definitely needed some rest. Even when they came to help us out, I didn't realize this nigga was this fucking crazy. What if things had gone different? How the fuck would he have explained that shit.

My ass could have died, and it was all a test. This shit was gone be hard as hell, but I was determined to pass this shit. Even if I didn't do anything with my skills, it would make me feel like more of a man to have them. Don't get me wrong, I have never been afraid to shoot a gun. Hell, me and my brothers done had to kill a lot of niggas. That was the problem. I've never killed on my own, and I'm not sure I have it in me to do so. I want to be cut from the same cloth as them niggas. Shit, I want mother fuckers to fear me when they see my ass. They feared me in a Hoover kind of way. Now these niggas were gone feel me in a Shadow kind of way. Starting with my wife.

The nagging and the bitching just won't stop. If she was one of my brother's wives, her ass would be scared to talk to me the way that she has. Trying to push it off as the hormones, I ignored most of it. The shit was starting to feel like Shirree all over again, and I was not about to deal with that shit. As soon as I got out the shower, she started in.

"Is this the kind of father you're going to be? In and out all times of night. Coming in beat the fuck up, with scratches and bruises, but no explanations. I'm not about to deal with this shit." I swear the shit was sounding like a broken record.

"Kimmie, shit gone be good. It's nothing going on with me. Just shit I have to handle. I promise we good."

"What kind of bitch do you think I am? Do you think I'm the type of bitch to take this shit lying down?" Finally reaching my breaking point, I snapped.

"You're the type of bitch that stays with a nigga that's beating your ass. You're the type of bitch that didn't say a fucking word. You're the type of bitch that's pissing me the fuck off." Before she could respond, I walked out the door and got in my car. I didn't even give a fuck what she had to say behind that shit. Did I go too far, fuck yea. I was tired of her shit, and a nigga didn't have to deal with that. Heading over to mom's house, I needed to get some kind of advice. There was no way I could talk to my brothers, and she was the only other choice I had.

Pulling up to her house, I made sure I rung the bell. My mama was a nasty nigga and I wasn't with her shit today. I needed to clear my mind not see some shit I didn't want to. When she opened the door, it was good to see her ass in some clothes. That meant I could probably get some good advice from her ass.

"Hey baby, what you doing here?" Giving her a hug, I sat down on the couch.

"I need some advice." Sitting down, she nodded at me to go head. "You know how everybody looks at me as the lil brother that just does whatever my brothers want me to do. Well, I'm tired of being lil Shadow Hoover. I know we supposed to be retired, but I've been training with Gangsta."

"The nigga that pours acid on coochie?" She actually crossed her legs and tried to cover herself up as if he was here.

"Mama, he pours acid on everything, not just coochie. Yea, but that's neither here nor there. I need to do this for me. I'm insecure about myself and I just want to feel that power my brothers feel. Not just because I'm a Hoover."

"It seems like you already got it worked out, so what's the problem."

"Kimmie ass. We been arguing left and right. Part of the training is me not telling anybody I'm in training. Her ass thinks I'm cheating and the shit driving me crazy."

"Speaking of Kimmie, she came by the other day mad as hell. Girl sat there and ate all my damn food. Bitch acted like she had two throats she had to feed. I don't even think I saw her chew, but she damn sure was swallowing.

Your ass must love her. The way she was swallowing down them biscuits, I know she gotta be taking your shit down whole. What? Don't look like that, I'm your mother and I know you weren't that blessed.

It's okay baby just tell them it's because it's curved. If you were straight it would be longer. You lucky your brothers started calling you Shadow, I used to call you pistol P." This lady could never stay on track.

"Ma, can we get back on the subject at hand?"

"Bitch don't get mad at me your shit stuck on your thigh. Ok Limpy look, I get why you are doing this. It's easier for others to tell you that you don't need to because they didn't have to live in the background of your brother's shadow. You get the training you need and do what you need to. Just don't get your dumb ass killed. As far as your wife, she ain't going nowhere.

When you at home, do you what you have to do to make her feel secure. Then go in the streets and do what you feel you have to do to be that man you trying to be. You have to learn how to balance that shit. I know you need this, but your wife doesn't know what is going on. She's pregnant and emotional. Hungry as fuck too, so feed her and fuck her. She will be alright." Everything my mom said made sense. Even though she kind of got off track.

"Thank you ma, and please don't tell nobody about this. I'm not trying to piss off Lucifer."

"Get the fuck out of my house. You done pissed me the fuck off. Mama ain't no snitch bitch. I might tell some stuff here and there, but I ain't no damn snitch. Fuck out of here." Looking at her like she was crazy, I got up to leave. How the fuck you gone say you ain't a snitch, but you will tell. Giving her a hug, I got out of there while I still could.

Running to the jewelry store, I grabbed Kimmie some diamonds and got her some food. It was time I made up with my wife. I know she don't know what's going on with me, but I need her to feel secure in my life.

Training was about to start, and it was only going to get harder. My ass was gone be MIA a lot, and I needed my girl to know ain't another bitch out there for me. Half of the reason Shirree didn't respect me was because of this. She felt I wasn't on the same level as my brothers. I couldn't allow that shit to happen with Kimmie. I loved her ass and I had to make sure she knew it through this process.

Walking in the house with the bags, I gave her the jewelry first. She gave me a half smile, but I could tell she was still pissed at me. I knew what I said was below the belt, but I was feeling attacked.

"I'm sorry Kimmie, I love you and I need you to know that. You fucking with my mental and the shit I'm dealing with, I can't have that. I need for us to be good. You gotta know I ain't going no fucking where." Giving her the food, her face lit up then.

"You should have led off with the food. I love you too baby. Thank you. I love my food." Her ass tossed the jewelry to the side and dived in her plate. If I would have known that would do the trick, I could have saved that ten thousand dollars. I'm glad we were good, because I had no idea what G had in store coming forward. Shit was about to get real.

CHAPTER 8 GANGSTA

Giving Shadow time to get his shit together, I didn't bring him in to train for a month. Even though it was Christmas season, I felt it was the perfect time for him to train. It was the best way to teach him to cut off his feelings. That would always be step one, and that was one step I wasn't sure he would be able to take.

The plane had been arranged for me to go to Chicago, but after this trip, his ass would be coming out here. His ass wanted to train, he would be the one to do the traveling. It was something that needed to be handled there, and it was the only reason I was going.

Grabbing my bags, my ass headed back to the airport. On top of the shit I had going on with Shadow, I was still doing hits from time to time. On top of all that shit, I still had to be a husband and a father. I could see why Suave didn't care about retiring. This shit can be draining, and I was tired. Preparing myself for this long flight, I got settled and took my ass to sleep.

As soon as I arrived, I headed straight to the house I needed to be at. Checking the door knob, I was irritated the shit was lock. It's been a while since I picked a lock and it was cold as fuck out here. After about two minutes, I got the shit opened and headed in.

Pulling my gun, I looked around trying to locate my target. Making my way to the den, the nigga was in the kitchen dancing while he ate a sandwich. That's some hungry shit Smalls would do. Creeping up behind him, all he cared about was taking a bite and never saw me coming. Knocking him out, I dragged him to the car. Tired as fuck, I drove to the warehouse. This was a lot of work a nigga was putting in over somebody's ego. Shadow ass better be worth it, or I would kill him myself and act like I don't know what happened.

Dragging the nigga inside, I set up the table and tied him to a chair. After I was done, I set up all the options and waited on Shadow to walk through the door. This nigga had five minutes to get here, or we were going to have a problem. Two minutes later he walked in the door. A prompt nigga, I like that shit.

"What are we doing here? I thought we were going to be training. I'm done with the games and shit, I barely made it out of your last sick ass test." This nigga was testy today. I guess I'll let him make it since he did almost die.

"This is training. It's steps to this shit and if you knew everything it was to know, we wouldn't be here. You know I do shit different, that's why you came to me. It's my way, or no way."

"Nigga don't act like you ain't out here jeopardizing my life. That's not how it's done. I want you to train me, not almost get me killed. It has to be another way to do this shit, or we can do it like a normal mother fucker would. Either way, something has to change." Purse dog thought he was bossing up on me.

"Forget about everything you thought you knew. All the things you have done means nothing at this point. Mother fuckers only feared you because of your

ST. JOHN THE BAPTIST PARISH LIBRARY
2920 NEW HIGHWAY 51
LAPLACE, LOUISIANA 70068

last name. I'm going to make it to where mother fuckers fear the thought of you."

"That's all good, but just make sure my brothers don't find out about this. We are retired, and the Hoover Gang roll together. It's either all of us, or none of us."

"Look, that's your family shit. When I'm done training you, your family won't even recognize who the fuck you are. From this moment on, you will turn off all feelings. Your brothers, child, and wife included. Do you think you can do that?" Shadow was worried, but that wasn't my job.

"Why the fuck do I have to turn off my feelings towards them? I get turning off my feelings and shit, but my brothers, wife, and kids. How the fuck does that work?"

"In order to be a God, you have to first be the devil. People will use your weakness. Family and friends are weaknesses. They will use that against you. If you are not ready for this, then we can walk away now. Everybody can't be Lucifer. I get that. The choice is yours to make. If you say yes, you have to do everything I say. What's it gone be purse dog?"

"I'm in." This was going to be hard because he loved the fuck out of his brothers. Once he figured out how to turn them off and completed training, I would teach him how to turn it on and off. I went ten years without showing Paradise anything, and it almost cost us our relationship. It's a time and place for everything, and I had to learn that shit.

"Good, now come over here and grab a knife." He did as he was told and walked over to me. Opening the door, he saw the nigga that was tied to the chair.

"What the fuck bro. What did our security do?"

"Nothing. It's part of your test. Now, quit asking questions and take the skin off this nigga until there is nothing left." You could see in his eyes, he wasn't with this shit. "When we were at the club, he allowed those niggas to get close to us. They got in with guns and fired on you niggas in your own shit. That falls on your security. I know you fuck with him, and that is why he is your first test. You know he fucked up and deserve to die, but your feelings is what's keeping you from wanting to do it. Over there on that table you have some options. You can use your knife and peel his skin off, or you can use another method. It's up to you." Purse dog walked over to the table and looked at what was there. Gasoline, gun, hammer, and a saw. This would show me what he was most comfortable with, and next time I would use something else.

He grabbed the hammer and walked over to his homie. I'm not gone lie, I was a little disappointed he chose the easy way out. The moment he started hitting dude in his head, I had to rethink that shit. By the third hit, it was like something inside of him snapped. I don't know if he was trying to be like me, or if this nigga was just as crazy as us. Either way, his ass went nuts. The guy's head was now torn from his body, and I would have assumed he would have stopped. This nigga grabbed his knife and started to peel the skin off his leg.

If I wasn't Lucifer, the shit would have turned my stomach and had me all fucked up in the head. Instead, I picked up the chain saw and proceeded to help him. Even though he has a monster inside of him, it only comes out when pushed. His first choice should have been to grab the knife or the saw. His fear is still what shows first, and that is what I needed to change.

It wasn't about making the nigga sick like me. It was about making him so ruthless, nobody knew what the fuck he would do. Fear is what he wanted, and fear is what I would give him. Once he figured out what he was good at, that would be his thing. Grabbing him away from the bones that was left, I looked into what used to be his eyes.

"Good job Purse dog, but that's enough for now. We have a long road ahead of us, and it will plenty more. Go home and get some rest. I will have this cleaned up." Nodding his head, he walked off. He would be alright, if not, oh fucking well. Grabbing my phone, I called Smalls.

"Hey nigga, I need a clean up crew at the warehouse and hurry the fuck up. I need to get back home to my girl."

"What crew bitch? You killed all they ass. Who the fuck imma send over there, some janitors?" Laughing, I hadn't thought about that.

"Well get your ass over here and help me."

Hanging up, I waited for Smalls to get there. I knew it wouldn't take long because that nigga was efficient. Fifteen minutes later, he was walking through the door eating a burger. "You stopped to get something to eat first?" He looked at me like I asked something wrong.

"What the fuck was I supposed to eat, ankles? Maybe yall left some ass cheeks. Yall never skin the back. Nasty ass niggas cutting off everything but dingaling, and you want me to be on an empty stomach." Walking over to what was left of the body, I grabbed the nigga's dick and cut it off.

"You ready now? Can we proceed?"

"You one sick ass nigga. They told me you eat people. Imma start staying in the room and watch your ass when you skinning them. Let me find out your ass in here with a hard dick and a full stomach. Been eating cheekbones and assholes. You know it's not chittlings if it's from a human right?" Rubbing my hand down my face, I swear you had to have patience dealing with our people.

"Nigga if you don't get your dumb ass over here and help me clean this shit up."

"You right. My bad." We laughed and cleaned the warehouse up. Even though it was abandoned and out the way, we always had to be careful.

"Sorry about your men, but you need to regroup fast as hell. We never want to be left exposed."

"Aight nigga I got you. I'm out." We both went our separate ways and I headed back to the airport. A nigga was tired as hell. I wonder how many people thought I ate niggas. That shit was funny as fuck. It was always good to hear new shit about myself. Everyone speculated on the type of nigga they thought I was. How do you explain the devil? I didn't think you could, but people still tried. Now they would do the same with Shadow. Let the games begin.

CHAPTER 9 SHADOW

"Bitch if you don't bring your ass over to the house, imma set your kitchen on fire. You know your wife ain't gone be able to take that shit and divorce your ass. I still think she ate my eyebrow off that night. Lips was looking mighty hairy. Mouth looking like Shepherd's Pie." Blaze always say some crazy shit, but I was lost on this one.

"Nigga what the fuck do Shepherd's Pie have to do with a hairy lip?"

"Nigga cus that shit is dog. Mother fuckers out here eating dog and shit. Dogs are hairy, your wife ate my brow, so her ass look like she eating... Look nigga that's neither here nor there. Your wife out here eating pubics bottom line. Get your ass over here so we can talk about Christmas." The way my training has been going and G not wanting me to show feelings, I was sure my ass wasn't gone be around for Christmas. Since I couldn't tell them that, I was going to the meeting.

"I'm on the way and have some food. Kimmie ass mean as hell if she hungry." His ass laughed, but we both knew the shit was true. Hanging up the phone, me and Kimmie headed out the door to go to Blaze's crib. I knew this was leading her on, but if I told her now, all hell would break loose.

"Are we going to be okay?" We couldn't go a day without her starting in on this shit.

"As long as you want to be. I'm here. Let's have a good day for once, and just maybe by the end of the night I could get some pussy." When she rolled her eyes, I knew that wasn't likely. I'm the only brother that barely gets any pussy, and I've always had a woman. This shit was getting old. Turning my radio up, I listened to *Kendrick Lamar* rapping bitch don't kill my vibe. It wasn't intentional, but the shit fit like a mother fucker.

My ass damn near jumped out the car and ran in Blaze's house. Usually I would open her door, but not today. I ain't have time. My brothers were always good for a laugh, and I needed that shit. It was going to be hard turning off my feelings towards them. Everybody knows how we roll, and I wasn't sure they would buy that shit.

"It's about damn time. Where Bertha?" This nigga was trying to make sure I didn't get no pussy.

"I got your Bertha. Fuck with me if you want to." I don't know why Kimmie insisted on trying to go toe to toe with Blaze. That nigga had no chill and no morals. No matter how much I trained, I still wasn't fucking with that nigga.

"Can we have a good day? Where the food at?" Giving Blaze a knowing look, he laughed and walked off to the kitchen. Nigga came back ten minutes later with a plate for Kimmie. Hearing her moan while she ate proved my point. Blaze was laughing too hard, and I knew his ass was on some bullshit.

"Shit good huh Kimmie?" Her ass barely looked up at Blaze.

"Fuck yeah. What is it."

"Sponge cake." The nigga fell to the floor laughing so hard, I knew he had did some shit. Walking over to her plate, I tried to grab it. She was so into the food, her ass hit me. Snatching it away from her, I looked at it closely.

"Kimmie come on now. You couldn't tell you was eating some bullshit? Blaze, what the fuck is this?" His ass could barely get it out he was laughing so hard.

"The sponge from under the sink dipped in syrup. Sponge cake. Give Bertha her meal back. You gone eat your cornbread looking ass." Kimmie hormones must have gotten the best of her, because she jumped up and ran out crying.

"Nigga you play too damn much. Come at my girl again I'm gone fuck you up. Try me if you want to."

Nigga threw his hands up to his neck like he was clutching his pearls. I thought he would take me seriously.

"All I know is my door better still be there. You know she eat anything. I wonder if that bleach and dish washing liquid gone give her the runs?" Ready to knock his ass out, Baby Face intervened.

"Aight yall that's enough. Blaze leave Bertha, I mean Kimmie alone. I'm sure she only ate the doorknob. Now let's start this damn meeting." These niggas had me fucked up. Grabbing a wad of money out of my pocket, I smacked they ass in the face with it.

"That should cover whatever we owe for Christmas. Me and my girl gone get up out of here.

Clown ass niggas." Walking away, it felt good to stand up to they ass.

"This nigga done slapped me in my face with some money." You could hear Quick going off, but now it was my time to laugh. Until I felt something smack me in the back of the head. Seeing Blaze standing behind me, I knew he had did the most. Seeing the open pamper on the ground, I regretted rubbing the back of my head.

"Did you hit me with a shitty pamper?" This nigga goes too far.

"Nope, I hit you with the shit inside the pamper. You and your bitch come to my house with a shitty ass attitude, I thought I would help you out. Get the fuck out my shit before I forget you my brother."

"Put some of that effort into getting your daughter potty trained. The fuck she still doing in a pamper? Yet, you got time to play and shit."

"Shitty Shadow Walker, do it look like I'm playing? You got about ten seconds to walk out of whatever's left of my door. I dare you to drop some shit along the way when you leaving too. Clown ass adopted ass nigga." My brothers were looking at me like I was in the wrong, when his bitch ass was the one that's feeding mother fuckers cleaning supplies.

Slamming the door behind me, I got the fuck up out of there. Turning my feelings off towards them niggas might be easier than I thought. Blaze have fucked all them niggas up before, but he don't fuck with them like he do me. Baby Face and Quick just sit there and let the shit happen. I know it's more so for the reason that they scared of his ass too, but fuck that. I couldn't wait to go back to training. These niggas were gone feel me, and they were gone see I wasn't baby Shadow no more. Fuck them.

"I'm not coming over here for Christmas. I'm sick of your brother."

"Shut the fuck up. Yes you are. Stop trying to swing balls back and forth with him, and we won't be in this shit. Do too damn much." I may have been wrong for snapping on her, but I was sick of all they ass. Not to mention, if I'm gone for Christmas, I needed her to be around family. Knowing I wasn't getting no pussy tonight, I tried to remember if I had some lube at home.

"That's why your ass smell like shit. You wanna talk about some balls, grow some. Your brothers walk all over your ass."

"Maybe, but they fuck you up every chance they get. Imma have the balls to sit there and watch next time instead of defending your ass. Say something else, your spongy ass gone walk home." The only thought that came to mind was G would be proud of me. I turned them bitches off quick today.

CHAPTER 10 KIMMIE

This nigga Shadow been gone for three days, and I was over his bullshit. He could say what he wanted about the shit I put up with, but this was something I was not willing to do. Christmas was tomorrow, and I couldn't even get my husband on the phone. What kind of shit was that.

Just in case the nigga showed up, I still needed to have our Christmas presents for everybody else. The girls were on their way over there to pick me up, so we could head to the mall. I really didn't want to be bothered with them bitches either, but I was tired of being left alone. Hearing the horn blow, I knew they were outside. Grabbing my purse, I locked up and went outside to meet them. As soon as I got in the car, I was ready to change my mind. Them bitches were entirely too happy for my liking.

"Heeeyyyy bitch. Girl you are getting big. You would think you were having a girl though, you not carrying low like most boys." Juicy usually was the laid back one, but she was talkative than a mother fucker today.

"Don't matter, I don't care what it is."

"Damn, somebody in a pissy mood today. It's snowing outside, which means it's going to be a white Christmas. How can you not be happy about that?" Ash always had that condescending ass tone, and it was pissing me off.

"Maybe because I don't give a fuck. Can we just go, I really want to get this shit done and get back home?"

"Oh no bitch, you could stay your ass home or drive your own car. You will not talk to us like that in my shit. Now get your shit together, we are going to have a good day and you are going to like it." This baby and my hormones had me ready to treat Drea's life, but I sat back and closed my eyes.

This baby had me realizing I really didn't like these bitches. Hoping it was just my hormones, because I seemed to not care about anybody these days. We were cool until I got about five months pregnant. Everything irritated me, and I was tired of pretending. I damn sure was tired of pretending to be a happy wife. The Hoovers had issues, and I definitely was tired of their ass. Blaze was in a category all by himself. I hated that nigga, and how everybody feared him. The nigga had a lighter, get the fuck over it.

Shadow allowed that nigga to get away with too much, and I was his wife. He told me from the beginning he wouldn't help me with him, but I didn't think he was serious. I always assumed he was joking. Don't get me wrong, I didn't think my husband was weak. All they ass allowed Blaze to get away with the stupid shit. Paradise even shocked me, I took her for a bitch that would shoot a nigga.

Pulling up to the mall, we got out and headed in. They went one way, and I went another. I'll call them when I'm done to see where they are. Right now, I just wanted to be by myself. Grabbing my husband a new Rolex, I picked up some stuff for the baby. Not sure if we were supposed to exchange gifts, I grabbed the girls matching Movado's, and his brothers some Giuseppes from him. Of course, I wasn't buying Blaze shit. I got that nigga some Sketchers, and I couldn't wait to see the look on his face. Getting something for the kids as well, I was done and ready to eat. Grabbing my phone, I called Drea to see where they were.

"Hey, are you all done? I'm finished, and my fat ass want to go to Pappadeaux."

"You got me fucked up. We will call you when we are done. Obviously, you didn't want to be with us, and now we don't want to be with your ass." This bitch got me fucked up.

"Look." Before I could say anything else, she hung up on my ass. This hoe sat mighty high on her pedestal, when she done went through brothers. Acting like her shit don't stank, and I was tired of it.

Knowing I couldn't do shit about it, I sat my big ass down on a bench. This was why I should have driven my own car, but I was trying to be lazy. Now, I'm stuck with a bunch of bitches that was getting on my nerves. Ugh I couldn't wait to have this baby. I didn't like anybody, and I knew they felt the same. Trying to call my husband one more time, I was shocked he answered.

"Hey, when are you coming home?" You could barely hear because his background was so loud.

"I'm trying to be home for Christmas, but I may not make it. I got you a gift though." Feeling the tears well up in my eyes, I needed to know what the fuck was going on.

"Shadow, where are you? It doesn't sound like you are working to me."

"I'm at the club." Looking at the clock, it was ten thirty in the morning. What the fuck club was he in. "Shadow, there is no club open here this early."

"I'm not in the US. Look, I gotta go the girls are about to give lap dances, and the guys say I'm killing the mood. I'll see you when I get back." Just like that, he hung up in my face. I couldn't stop the tears from flowing, and I was mad as hell. When he gets back, we were going to have a long talk. If this was the type of husband he was going to be, I wanted no parts of this shit.

"Kimmie, what's wrong babes? I'm sorry for how I talked to you. I just wanted to get you back for how you were treating us. We can go to Pappadeaux." Drea was back to being the sweetheart everyone thought she was.

"Me and Shadow are having problems, and I'm sorry I have been taking it out on everybody. This baby got me mean as hell, but I don't know how to stop it." My shit was all over the place, and I had no idea what to do with these feelings.

"It's okay bitch. We all have been there. Let's go get you some food and you should be happy again. Wait, we can't go get seafood, you can't eat that. We taking your ass to Gibson's and you gone eat and be happy." Ash rubbed my tears away and pulled me up from the bench. I really didn't give a fuck where we ate, my ass craved everything. All the damn time.

"Let's go, and I'm not paying either. Grabbing my bags, we headed back towards the car. I was happy all the gifts were going to Blaze's house, and I didn't have to carry all that shit in the house.

The rest of the day went good and I actually had fun. We laughed while they drunk liquor, and I ate everything under the sun. I was in a happy place, and I couldn't wait to get home and go to sleep. We had been hanging for about ten hours, and these dogs were barking bitch take your ass home. When they pulled up to the house, I damn near skipped in. Shadow was standing there looking sexy as hell.

CHAPTER 11 GANGSTA

Standing on the open field, I knew that I had to train this nigga on shooting. He barely hit one of my men, and his ass was letting it ride. This nigga wasn't scared, but he couldn't shoot to save his life. Shadow's plane had landed, and I was waiting on the nigga to arrive.

He walked up trying to figure out what the hell was going on. It was three men tied to a tree. Each in different positions on the field. One was closer, one was further away, and one in the middle. His ass was gone learn to shoot today. The men that was tied up were a hit that I had to do. The client didn't care how I killed them, they just wanted them gone. Why not put they ass to good use?

"What the fuck is this?" Laughing, I walked him over to the table of guns. I would allow him to use what he was comfortable with at first, and then I would push him out of his comfort zone.

"Target practice. You can't shoot for shit my nigga. If I had not of been there, your ass would be cooked. Now, use the gun you are most familiar with. Aim for the person that's closest to you." Grabbing the gun, he did what I asked. This nigga let off an entire clip and didn't hit shit. "Concentrate. We are not about to be here all day. Clear your head and aim for the target."

"What the fuck you think I'm doing? I'm trying."

"You're not trying hard enough. Do you really think you can do what I do shooting like this? You need to focus. Tunnel vision. The only thing you see is him." The nigga reloaded with an attitude, but I had time. Pointing his gun at the target, he took a deep breath. This time he hit him in the leg and stomach.

"I hit him." His ass was actually excited.

"You happy? It just took you five minutes to hit him in his leg and shit. His ass can still raise his gun and kill you. Your tunnel vision need to click in faster, and you need to be proficient." Slamming a new clip in the gun, Purse dog appeared to be pissed. Trying not to laugh in his face, I moved back and let him do his thing. This time, he fired off quicker, but he barely hit him.

Not saying shit else, he reloaded and fired again. His anger was making him better. I had to figure out a way to channel that shit all the time.

"Quick would have laid these niggas out in ten seconds flat. What you doing Purse dog?" That must have triggered him, because this time he tore the nigga's head off.

"Is that good enough for you?" Slamming the gun down, he thought he was done.

"It was cute and all but pay attention." Grabbing a gun off the table, I continued to stare at Purse dog. Pointing my gun towards the trees, I fired three shots. Without even looking, I knew I hit all of them in the head. The look on his face told me so. "Your anger helps you unleash a beast, but you need to figure out a way to keep that with you at all times. You shouldn't be pushed into a monster. You have to learn how to turn the shit on and off. You're training, so when you out there, use what people say and those feelings to be that monster. I'll teach you how to turn it on and off later."

Nodding, he reloaded his gun and pointed. You could see his jaw line moving and I knew he was thinking about shit that pissed him off. This time, he got two chest shots and one head shot. Looking at me smiling, I could see he was proud. His ass thought the shit was over though.

"Now I need you to grab a gun you are not comfortable or familiar with. You need to learn how to shoot anything, and anybody." Grabbing a shot gun, you could see him making his self pissed off. Pointing the gun, he tore threw they ass. This was good. We accomplished a lot today, and it didn't even take long. Once I taught him the mental, Shadow was gone be alright.

"You did good Purse dog, let's go celebrate."

"It's almost Christmas, can I go home and come back for training?" Looking at him like he was crazy, I laughed.

"Nigga what the fuck is Christmas? That shit dead now. We going to the strip club like I said. Go get dressed." He was pissed but did what I asked.

We all met up at the club, and the shit felt good. It was me, Suave, Shadow, and some nigga named Kip that Suave was cool with. Even though we were in Hawaii, they knew how to turn the fuck up. We were drunk off our asses, and the ladies were looking good than a mother fucker. Right when we decided to get lap dances, Shadow's phone rung.

"You think that nigga could really be you? Your eyes would go black and I knew you checked out. Hell, I don't even possess that shit. You and Paradise are the only two people that I've seen able to do that shit."

"I'm not sure if he will be able to turn his feelings off, but that nigga damn sure got a monster inside of him. He has to be pissed to bring it out, but it's there. Nigga shocked the shit out of me." Just as me and Suave was saying we didn't know if he could turn his feelings off, Shadow shocked us again.

"I'm not in the US. Look, I gotta go the girls are about to give lap dances, and the guys say I'm killing the mood. I'll see you when I get back." The nigga hung up and me and Suave damn near passed out from laughing. His ass definitely deserved an award.

"Hey, bring the bitches over here, I got a couple of lap dances in me. Purse dog, gone and go home. Be back before training at three in the afternoon. If you are one minute late, you will regret it. I'll text you the address." The nigga was drunk but managed to run his ass up out of there. Even though he loved his wife, he disrespected her in front of company. That was his way of turning off his feelings. I didn't even have to coach him to do it. Lil nigga was learning.

"Baby brother, you might be on to something. This nigga just snatched Kimmie's soul. Paradise had to beat your ass for you to get it."

"Fuck you nigga. I fought back." Everybody laughed, including me. I'm not gone lie, Paradise knocked a booger out my ass the first time I fucked up. I was looking forward to beating on Purse dog, but he was surprising the shit out of me.

I couldn't wait for training tomorrow. This nigga was gone be a monster, and I was determined to make it happen. My phone went off, and I saw that it was Paradise texting me.

Crazy P: Bring your ass home now, or I'm slapping you to sleep.

Laughing, I got up and called it a night. I was too tired to fight, and I wasn't taking no L's. Paradise would fuck around and get shot today.

CHAPTER 12 SHADOW

I know I pissed Kimmie off when I said that shit to her, but I had to. Anything could be a test with G, and I wasn't about to get dropped from my training over some stupid shit. I felt bad as hell, and I was glad Gangsta allowed me to go home to make it right.

My ass damn near flew to the airstrip to get on that plane. I had to stop by the hotel to get her gift, and I was on my way. She was pissed, but I knew my girl would be happy to see me. My dick was hard each time I hit one of their bodies. That adrenaline had me ready to fuck the shit out of my wife.

As soon as the plane landed, I made my way home. She wasn't there when I made it, but I sat in the front room waiting on her. When I heard the door open, the look of happiness on her face really made me feel like an ass. She ran to me and in that moment, I didn't give a fuck about anything else. Pulling her pants down, she stepped out of them and I took over. Picking her up around my waist, I used my free hand to pull my dick out.

"I missed you so much baby. I'm so glad you're home."

"Shut the fuck up and take this dick." You could tell she was shocked but turned on at the same time. Her ass started bucking, and I was turned on like a mother fucker.

"Damn baby that hook. Shit." She was going crazy like the bitches were doing over Safaree. Now I don't know what that nigga was packing, but it feels good when a chick is acting like you the biggest thing slanging. Gripping her around her waist, I tore into her guts like it was the last piece of pussy a nigga was getting.

"Didn't I say shut the fuck up? Take this dick like I know you can, and don't say another fucking word."

"Okay daddy." This mother fucker was hard headed, but I was about to show her ass today. Leaning her head all the way to the couch, I brought her hips close to mine. Slamming into her pussy, I could see her clit swelling up. I wanted to rub that mother fucker, but she was too damn big to be holding with one hand. She would never forgive me if I dropped her.

She must have been really missing a nigga, because her ass squirted all over this dick. That shit drove me crazy, it was no better feeling than that right there. When I kept pushing this curve on her spot, she went crazy and squirted again. If she wasn't already pregnant, her ass was going to be tonight. Shooting my seeds inside of her, my girl's walls swallowed the shit out of them mother fuckers.

I couldn't stop shaking from that nut, and I was loving every minute of it. This was why I married her, and I was never letting her go. Carrying her weak body up the stairs, I laid her in the bed. She was gone have to get in the shower when she got her energy back, but I got her a towel and washed her down.

Jumping in the shower, I was in a good mood. Shit was starting to look up, and I was feeling good about myself. It was going to be a different story in a few hours. There was no way she wasn't going to go off, when she found out I had to leave back out. Even though the right thing to do would be to wake her up, I was going to slip the fuck up out of here. That's an argument I could save for another day. Easing out in the room, I got dressed as quietly as possible. My intentions were to lay down, but it might be best this way.

As soon as I slid my feet in my shoes, her ass woke up. You would think I had a piece of meat dangling in front of her nose. My ass felt like a nigga got caught stealing her snacks from under her pillow.

"Where are you going baby? You don't have to get me any snacks, I got a drawer full."

"I have to go back. I'm not done handling business, but as soon as I'm done I'm running back to your fine ass." Her ass shot up in that bed like she was ready to knock my ass out.

"Some stripper bitch turned you on, you came home fucked me, and now you leaving? If you walk the fuck out of that door, don't bring your ass back."

"Don't start that shit Kimmie. I love you, and I came home because I missed you. I promise I will be back as soon as I am done. When it is all over, I promise you will understand. Just bear with me." Bending down to kiss her, I rubbed her face, and headed out the door. She was upset now, but all she had to do was trust me and we would be alright.

****

I made it back just in time and G wouldn't be upset. Looking at my phone, I headed to the address that he texted me. When I got there, it was nothing in sight but a field. This nigga loved the outside, and I was paranoid that someone would see us. Looking around, I realized nothing was around here and I felt more comfortable. G was standing there with a guy laying on a table. It was a bunch of stuff that you could use to burn some shit up. I had no idea what he had planned.

"What is this shit? You know this is not my thing. What are we training with today?" He laughed at me.

"You told me you were tired of living in your brother's shadow. Instead of training to be like them, I decided to train you to be better. They each have a thing that they are good at. Nobody steps into the other's territory. I'm training you to know all of their trades. You will be able to do anything that anyone of them can do.

Yesterday you were Quick. Today, you are Blaze. Are you ready?" This was some bullshit on another level.

"I'm not trying to get inside of that nigga's head. He does the fucking most."

"I agree, but that nigga can do shit with fire that nobody can. You will learn to be that nigga. Not that goofy shit, but the shit he can do with fire. Now, over there on the table are some things you can use. Take your pick." Walking over to the table, I started to pick up the gasoline. It was easy and quick. I knew he was testing everything I do.

Grabbing the blow torch, I walked over to the nigga and started to melt his face. It was getting easier to channel my anger. All I had to do was make myself hear all the shit talking from over the years. I know my brothers loved me, but they treated me different. They thought I wasn't strong enough to do shit. Even when we were robbing banks, they ass would leave me in the car. Never any respect. The madder I got, the more I burned. Placing the blowtorch back on the table, I grabbed the acid and started to pour it on his dick.

Taking it to his face, what was left of it, I continued to pour. Thinking about all the mother fuckers that tried me, I walked back over to the table and grabbed the lighter. Instead of using the gas, I held the shit to his body parts. His screams didn't scare me or turn me off, they made my adrenaline pump.

"Purse dog, slow down my nigga. It's all good. The nigga didn't fuck your bitch. He was just stealing a couple of dollars here and there." G poured gas on the guy and lit him up. “Come on, we can go now. You did your job. Nigga you starting to scare me. Your ass may be getting crazier than me. Let me find out your ass the real Lucifer, and you been playing our ass.”

“Naw, I’m just lil ol purse dog trying to get taught by the best. Just the fact that you can teach me all this, proves that. Now can I go home?”

“Even though you will miss Christmas, you can go. I’ll let you know when I need you back.” Smiling, I felt good about myself. Heading home with a hard on, I couldn’t wait to get back to Kimmie.

CHAPTER 13 KIMMIE

It's been a rough couple of months, and I didn't think me, and my man would make it through. This nigga was going missing at the drop of a dime. The nigga barely made it home for Valentine's Day. We had the biggest fight ever, but I left it alone because he showed up. The only thing that I regretted was the fucked up shit I said to Drea, Juicy, and Ash. I basically told them their niggas was cheating, and they were stupid.

They were pissed, but I guess my words planted a seed. If they didn't feel the way that I did, they ass wouldn't have went off like they did. I'm not sure if Shadow was cheating, but he carried all of the signs. If his ass was cheating, then they ass was too.

I hate how I brought it to them, and I needed to make it up. Even though I still felt the same way, I shouldn't have come at them like that. They didn't say one word to me at Mama Debra's wedding. Me and Shadow barely said one word to each other for a month.

We were just starting to get to a good place, but I think it's only because it's almost time for the baby to come. We had a couple of weeks left, but I had no idea if he would even be here. His ass was flaky as hell, and around when he wanted to be. At this point, I was all cried out. There were no more tears in me, and I was just ready to get this baby out of me.

"Kimmie, are you ready to go? We're late and you know how I am about time?" Grabbing my jacket, I headed downstairs. We were going over to Baby Face's house for the get together, and even though I didn't like Blaze ass, this would be my chance to apologize to my girls. It's been lonely as hell with Shadow gone all the time.

"I'm ready." We got in the car and drove over. As soon as we walked in the door, Blaze started in.

"The last time I saw you, your ass ate my couch and shit. Sit your ass down somewhere and wait until the food is done. Loosey, get Kimmie some snacks, I ain't got no more nipples and shit. She will bring you something in a minute." Shadow pushed him out the way, and I ignored him. I wasn't giving him the satisfaction today. Walking over to the girls, I figured now was a good time to say I'm sorry.

"Don't leave your man alone, I might slip on his dick. Since I'm the whore of the group and all." Drea didn't even let me get the shit out, before she started in, but I knew why she was doing it.

"Look, I'm so sorry for the things I said to you all. Even though I believe all they ass could be cheating, it wasn't fair for me to say those things to you all. Yall the only damn friends I got, and it's been lonely as hell."

"Bitch those tears don't move me, you said some fucked up shit. Now I'm gone forgive you, but don't let the shit happen again." Juicy was always the tough one.

"Kimmie fuck are you crying for? I'm surprised you didn't lick the bitches off your cheeks. You must have had something to eat before you walked in." Blaze just didn't know when to let shit go.

"Blaze, fall back. I'm not on that shit with you. Not today." Shadow has been defending me a lot lately, and the shit made me feel good. If only his cheating ass stayed home.

"Baby you had three hens, no more. Not today. Baby you ate the entire goose, no more. Not today. See how easy that shit is to say, try saying that shit to your girl. Mother fucker done ate so many animals imma start calling her ass mother goose. Nigga walk past me she mooing and shit. Fuck out my face." You could tell Shadow was getting pissed, but I was here to fix shit with my girls.

"I promise, the shit will never happen again. Besides, I can't be mad at my baby's God mothers. I need all you bitches there." Looking at Shadow, I tried to whisper. "Yall know that nigga might not be here for the shit." We all laughed and started having an inside joke at his expense. The doorbell rung, and we assumed it was Mama Debra. Everyone kept talking until some fine ass nigga walked in. Me and the girls looked at him and tried to figure out where the fuck he came from.

"Everybody, this is our umm brother Zavic." The quiet in the house was eerie. Drea leaned towards us and cracked a joke.

"I'm glad he wasn't around in my slipping days. A bitch may have slipped." Juicy pushed her in the back of the head while we laughed.

"Baby Face what the fuck are you talking about? Nigga pants tight as hell, ain't no way he a Hoover. Chuck Norris, can you give us a minute to talk?" The fine nigga laughed and walked out. This shit was juicier than a steak medium rare.

“He said Rico is his father. His mother just told him since she found out he was dead. He paid her to keep her silence, but now that he is gone, she can talk.”

“Ladies give us a minute. We need to figure this shit out, and you know we don’t conduct business in front of you.” Quick ass had to be the thinking one. We walked out, but we leaned against the kitchen door to listen. They had us fucked up.

CHAPTER 14 BLAZE

As much shit as I had to say, I am actually speechless. This nigga just shows up out of nowhere talking about he our brother. We don't do outsiders, but how the fuck do we turn away a Hoover. We weren't built like that. Just because our father was fucked up, don't mean we had to take the shit out on that nigga. This was one hell of a dilemma. We had been through too much to go through some bullshit now.

"Chuck, let me get this straight. Your mom was getting paid off to not say anything. Our father was pronounced dead years ago, why didn't she say anything then?" Baby Face was usually the thinker, but Shadow was on his shit today. That was a damn good question.

"You will have to ask her that. All I know is she just came to me a few months ago, and I had to do a lot to find you. If you don't want me here, that's cool. You don't want to accept your father was fucking all over the place, that's fine too. Just know I'm out here and you not the only Hoover." The nigga was trying to get smart.

"Well duh bitch. You ever heard of Larry? Hell naw that nigga ain't one of us. Let me guess, you the slow one?"

"Naw I'm the one that loves to torture. You want to try me?" Oh this nigga thought he was tough. I flicked my Bic and I was about to take this nigga entire lining.

"Calm down Blaze. Where is your mom now? If we chose to talk to her, could you arrange that?" Nodding his head yes, we all looked at each other. That means this nigga might not have been lying. This was fucked up. Whether the nigga was telling the truth or not, I would never accept his ass. Loosey could wear the pants this nigga had on.

"This is hard for us. We don't allow new people in our circle. We been through too much. I'm telling you now, if I find out you on some bullshit, I will shoot you myself. I promise I won't miss. If you don't know what you are up against, you might want to do your research. The Hoovers aren't to be fucked with, even if your blood is the same as ours. Fuck with us, you won't fuck with nobody else." Quick was pissed and I wish I could take him seriously. The entire time he was going off, I kept watching the patch in his head moving. Spark fucked that nigga up. It was growing in, but you could still see that shit. Funny thing is, Chuck didn't look bothered.

"Chuck leave us your number, and we will set something up to come and talk to you. We need to think about this." He gave Baby Face his number, and almost left peacefully. Until the devil in a bad wig walked in.

"Where the fuck the food at? I'm hungry as hell." Even though my mama was the first lady now, she still acted the same.

"Mama we kind of in the middle of something." Shadow nodded towards Chuck and my mama was about to start flirting. You could see the look in her eye. I had to stop her, I couldn't allow my mama to look like an incest whore in a bad wig.

"Chuck here says he is our brother. Rico is his father and paid his mama off to keep quiet." Mama head whipped around so fast.

"Ain't no way that's his son. Who in the fuck names their son Chuck? Tight ass visionary ass pants. Looking like Prince son on Sunday's only. Fuck out of here. Where the food at?" She stormed in the kitchen door and the girls all fell to the floor. "Look at this dumb shit here." Kicking them first, she stepped over them and went in the kitchen.

"I'm sorry about that Chuck. Mama is still a lil touchy on the subject of my father. As Baby Face said, we will call you after we have had time to process this." Shadow was being the responsible one again.

"Yall do know my name ain't Chuck. You can call me Vic. I'll be around."

"Nigga you are who we say you are." He left, and nobody knew what to say. No matter how many times we think our lives were going normal, something always happened. This nigga was up to something, and I didn't give a fuck what they said.

"He not getting in our circle. I don't trust nobody who just pops the fuck up in tight ass billie jeans. Fuck that shit."

"It's a good thing it ain't up to you then." Shadow's mouth was getting real slick, and I was two seconds away from lighting his ass up.

"You been gone lately, so let me refresh your memory. I'm that nigga. Brother or mother, I will fuck your bitch ass up. Keep playing tough, imma show you how soft your ass is. Nigga flammable than a mother fucker, but wanna talk shit." The look Shadow gave me almost made me shoot him for real. I've seen that look a lot over the years. Gangsta wore that look well. This nigga looked dead in the eyes. It didn't scare me, it just let me know that I had to watch his bitch ass.

"Whatever nigga. Kimmie, let's go."

"Yeah, get the fuck on. Maybe he could be our brother and replace your ass. You know we only allow four of us. You were adopted any fucking way. Adopta bitch. That's your new name." He practically dragged Kimmie out of there, and that was not easy to do. She was eight months pregnant and big as hell.

"Blaze, what I tell you about telling my son he was adopted? He just different. Leave him alone. Figure out what the fuck is going on with this thin ass nigga Chuck. If he was Rico's son, he might be a bitch." We all looked at each other.

"Mama we are Rico's sons too." She looked me dead in my fucking eye.

"Exactly."

"I was about to hug you, but that's why your wig stank. Funky ass cheap ass sheep dog. Don't get mad at us cus you don't know who your baby daddy is. Shadow ain't one of us." Even though I was pissed, I was just talking shit. I knew he was my brother, but he had me fish grease hot. I loved that sensitive ass nigga.

"Fuck you bitch. I swear sometimes I wish I had let you fall on the fucking sheets. You so damn extra. Get the fuck out of the way. I have to get to the church. The mother's board want me to pray for them." We all bust out laughing because she was dead ass serious.

"Blaze, you have to take it easy on Shadow. That's our baby brother. You have to stop doing him like that. Now let's figure this shit out about this nigga Chuck. We gotta figure this shit out quick." Everybody agreed with Baby Face, but nobody knew how the fuck we were supposed to figure it out.

"Aight yall, me and Loosey out of here. Quick, we gone meet yall back at the house. Since Spark still upstairs playing with the kids, bring her back with you for me."

"Nigga she burned my hair off. I don't want her sitting behind me, I don't trust her ass."

"Shid, she snitched on me, I don't trust her ass either. I'm trying to get some outdoor pussy. I need to fuck my girl quick. You saw how Chuck looked in them jeans. I need to make sure my girl remember what the fuck I got down there."

"I'm trying to fuck Ash tonsils loose. Her mouth juicy as fuck when she on her menstrual." We all high fived.

"You know we are standing right here? Nasty ass niggas." Ash tried to sound mad, but you could see the water dripping from the corners of her mouth. The shit was so juicy, I couldn't stop myself from looking.

"I'm not the one that fucked your girl, quit lusting over mine. Juicy name is self explanatory, gone and get his ass back." Baby Face looked like he wanted to kill Quick.

"Nigga she got PPD. I'm not trying to be on meds and shit fuck that. Juicy got that hot water. Fuck that."

"It's postpartum depression." Everybody screamed the shit like it was supposed to make a difference.

"What that mean, it goes away?" Everybody shook they head at me and laughed. I'm still missing the joke.

"Just gone Blaze. I'll bring Spark home. If I find a lighter on her, I promise she gone be on the side of the road." Shrugging my shoulders, I laughed as I pulled

Drea outside. I was about to get some pussy and I was not about to let anybody ruin that shit for me. As soon as we got in the car, I took my dick out. It crowded the car, but I needed some now.

"Come climb on this dick." As soon as she got her leg out, and got on top of me, Quick started banging on the window.

"You niggas nasty as a mother fucker, you could have least drove a block away. You knew damn well we were coming out here with these kids."

"Mannnn, fuck them kids." We all started laughing. "You right, let me drive off." Drea climbed back in her seat and I drove a block away. I was about to get this pussy.

CHAPTER 15 ZAVIC

Heading back to my hotel, I didn't know what to say about that meeting. You could tell they were shocked and knew absolutely nothing about me. The fact still remained I was Rico's son, and a Hoover. Whether they liked it or not, nothing was going to change that.

I've never been the one to kiss ass or try to make someone accept me, and I wasn't about to start now. They had all this time, and now it's mine. Quick told me to do my research, but I already had. I wanted to know who I was dealing with. I've been a loaner most of my life.

It's always just been me and my mom, with visits from my dad. I wanted to tell them we never knew he supposedly died the first time. He was around us, and that means he was more of a father to me than them. I don't know how they would feel about that, and that could really cause conflict between us.

My mom told me my dad named me Zavic Hoover, which I never understood since his name was Rico. I was twenty seven years old, and I never knew my brothers existed until a couple of months ago.

I was really surprised to see how well they had done in life. My guys pulled their bank statements, and they were living large. Using clubs to clean dirty money was brilliant, and I was sure that wasn't all of it. No street nigga would put all their money in a bank. Which says a lot about their finances. All of them had millions in their accounts.

My guy also told me there was a death certificate on Blaze at one point, but I'm not sure what happened there when he is obviously alive. There was no way for me to ask them that, without them knowing I ran their shit. They weren't the only Hoover that had connections. They were bank robbers, but I have been the biggest drug dealer Louisville had ever seen. I guess it ran in our blood. My phone rung, and I didn't recognize the number.

"Yeah, what's up."

"This is Baby Face, we are going to have a family gathering and you need to come. You will meet everybody officially."

"Just text me the date and time, I'll be there. Wait, how did you get my number?"

"You have your people, and I have mine. See you soon." Did this nigga know I ran a check on them? I should have known they were going to have me checked out. They don't trust nobody at this point. It was all good because everything about me would check out. I'm sure this gathering was going to be interesting, but I was looking forward to it. My phone rang again, and I was not in the mood for this call. Taking a deep breath, I answered.

"Hey, how did it go?"

"How did what go? I introduced myself and they took turns questioning me. The same shit I would have done had they come showing up at my door."

"Did they believe you? Are you in the circle?"

"Why wouldn't they believe me, it's the truth. Look, it's been a long day and we are meeting again soon. I'll call you after that. Right now, I'm going to finish learning who my brothers are and get some rest. I suggest you do the same."

"Who do you think you are talking to? I'm the reason you are even there. Let's not forget."

"You know who the fuck I am. Don't think we are in something together because we are not. I do not work for you, and I am not working with you. I said I'll be in touch. It will be in your best interest not to talk to me in that manner again. Have a good night." Hanging up the phone, I poured myself a drink and looked over the other file I had. I would get to the bottom of this, but on my own terms. Nobody was going to tell me what I should do, or how I should feel. I've never been that nigga a mother fucker could run or scare. That's why Quick's words didn't move me.

Funny thing is, I knew everything he was saying was the truth. He wasn't throwing idle threats, but he didn't know me. I was a force to be reckoned with. The jury was still out on if my brothers would feel that force.

CHAPTER 16 GANGSTA

Training with Shadow was finally done, and a nigga was kind of sad. I was getting used to him being around, and it felt good to have someone looking to me for answers. We had grown pretty close, and I never would have expected that shit. The only thing I wasn't sure on was his ability to turn his feelings on and off.

After what happened with me and Paradise, I can't completely force him to turn the shit off. That shit almost cost me everything, and I wouldn't want to see the same thing happen to him. Today was his first job, and I was going with him to make sure everything went smooth.

When he asked me to train him, I didn't know he wanted to go into the same profession as me. He was a grown as man, and he knows the consequences. I would look out for him like me and Paradise look out for each other while we are out there. The job he had to do tonight was an easy one. They didn't care how he died, they just wanted him gone.

He was a construction worker, and I had no idea what he did to piss someone off. That was never our concern. It wasn't our job to give a fuck, and I wasn't about to start today. I didn't ask how he planned to kill his target, but I wanted to watch. It was interesting that Shadow planned to kill him on his job.

Sitting in my car, I watched the target walk towards the port a potty. Shadow ran in ahead of him, and I laughed at the aggravation on the target's face. His ass looked like he had to shit something awful. Shadow walked out, and the target walked in. I was confused as I watched Shadow coming towards the car. Until the damn port a potty blew up. One thing I have never done was laugh during a kill, but my ass was in my stomach. I could not stop laughing at this nigga. Shit and body parts flew everywhere.

This had to be the funniest shit I seen in a long time. I don't know what kind of monster I created, but I was loving this shit. This nigga jumped in the car looking nonchalant, and I could not stop laughing. I was expecting him to do something simple on his first time.

"I can say this, you are no longer Purse dog. From this day forward, you have earned my respect lil nigga." Putting the car in drive, I took off.

"That means a lot to me, so I'm guessing I did good."

"Nigga you did great. You might be sicker than me in the head. I would hate to be the person that have to come work this crime scene. Shit and booty was everywhere." We laughed all the way back to my office. When we got there, I gave him his money. "Are you ever going to tell your brothers and wife what you are out here doing?" You could see the perplexed look on his face.

"It's always been the four of us out there. If they know I'm out here freelancing, it's going to be a problem."

"What you gone do when the baby comes?"

"I haven't thought that far ahead. Right now, I'm just trying to enjoy my freedom." Understanding that shit, I ended the conversation and let him leave. I was about to wrap the shit up, but I got an email. Checking it, I saw it was two jobs. One was for someone in Chicago, and one was in Texas. They both were for the same day. Not sure if Shadow was ready to do hits on the road, I chose to give him the one at home. That way he could do that shit and take his ass home to be with his wife.

Looking over the email, I almost changed my mind and took it for myself. There was no name or file on the target. They referred to him as the hit. Only stating where he would be, his description, and time I found that shit intriguing. It was something I would like to do because I liked challenges. Looking at the second email, it was for someone in politics. He was high profile, and I knew it was no way I could give Shadow that one. Grabbing my phone, I called Suave to see if he was willing to do the one in Texas.

"Bro, I need you to do a job for me. High profile and out of town."

"Not gone be able to do it. Tank moved us back to Chicago, but she is not letting me do jobs. The shit on Valentine's Day was a once in a lifetime thing." Looking confused, that shit sounded dumb as fuck to me.

"Let me get this straight, you were miserable in Hawaii and she brought you back to the streets just so you could look at them?" He laughed, but I didn't understand what the fuck was funny.

"I never said I was coming out of retirement. My ass was just tired of being there bored to death. I needed to be home."

"All you doing is being bored in Chicago. Look, it's two jobs in one day, and it's one I really want to take. I'm not sure if Shadow is ready for the road."

"I'm sorry baby bro I can't. If you didn't have someone else to do it, then I would have no choice. That's not the case though. Quit being a brat and do the one you know you have to." Not even bothering to say bye, I hung up the phone. I hated his ass sometimes.

Shadow was just gone get the interesting one, there was no way I was trusting him with a nigga that had constant security around him at all times. Fuck. Suave was right, I was just gone have to suck this one up.

Saturday was going to be curtains for a couple of people. I wish I could be there to see how Shadow was going to handle that one. I'll just make his ass tell me word for word what the fuck happened.

CHAPTER 17 QUICK

This shit with Chuck was driving me crazy. Shadow asked a legitimate question, and he never answered. Why are you showing up now, after all this time? Why not when he was dead all those years? This nigga shows up out the blue, and I don't think I'm willing to just accept him like that.

Me and Blaze seems to be the only one to agree. Shadow seems down with it, and Baby Face is always the reasonable one. Except when it came to Rico. That nigga did not want that nigga around. Even though me and Blaze went at each other a lot, we thought the same. I don't trust this nigga, and I don't want him around my family.

I don't even like the idea of his ass knowing where Face lives and we don't know how. I'm sure Face had our guy run his shit, but we had come too far to go through some more bullshit. All I wanted was to be happy with my fucking family. It seemed like we just couldn't get away from it, and I refused to allow this nigga to come in and disrupt our shit.

I started not to even attend this dumb ass dinner that Face set up. We bought out a restaurant and we all supposed to meet and talk there. My mama refused to come, so she had all the kids. We had an hour to get there, and Ash was taking forever. I didn't agree with the women being there, but Face said they needed to know what was going on just in case they needed to be prepared.

"Ash, will you come the fuck on. Why the hell do we always have to be the late ones? It's not hard, wash your ass and put on your clothes. I already don't wanna be there, so let's get this shit over with." Her ass didn't even respond so I walked in the bedroom. She had our shit looking like a hospital and I fell out laughing.

"Mr. Hoover the doctor thinks there is a problem with your scrotum, and I need to run a series of test. Can you get undressed and lay down on the bed please." We had to be at the place in an hour, and her ass wanted to role play.

"Ash, we have to go baby. I promise when we get back home, I'll let you check more than my scrotum."

"I'm sorry sir, but if you don't do this test, your life could be at risk. Please take off your clothes and lie down." Looking at my wife all sexy in her nurse uniform, I said fuck that shit. Chuck could wait. Taking my clothes back off, I climbed in the bed. "Okay, this will not hurt." She started pushing in places over my body. When she got to my dick, she checked it. As soon as she touched my shit, it got hard.

"Mr. Hoover, it seems you like your check up. I didn't know you were this endowed. I've never seen one this big before."

"Girl that's semi. If you want to see it at its full length put it in your mouth." She looked around to make sure no one was coming and slid it in her mouth. Her deep throats always killed me out, because women couldn't take me whole.

"We have to hurry up. A doctor may come in to check you." Lifting her dress, she climbed on top of me.

"I hope you not about to do that scoot shit. If you climbing up there, you gone ride this shit." Placing her hands against my chest, she sat on my dick as if she was squatting. When she started bouncing on my shit, I knew I wasn't gone last long. "Fuck girl, ride this dick." Ash kept doing some trick where she would just take the tip in, and then drop all the way down. Her pussy was soaking wet, and my dick was about to bust. Grabbing her by her hips, I rammed inside her shit until my nut worked its way up her walls.

"Alright nurse Betty, we gotta go. Wash that shit off and hurry the fuck up. Only you will get horny when we got somewhere to be."

"Your ass needed to bust a nut before you go here and kill this nigga. You were stressing, I helped you. Now let's go." We both jumped in the shower and finished fast as hell. Getting dressed in record time, we were on our way to the dinner.

****

The tension in the room was crazy. Nobody was talking and Kimmie came on behalf of Shadow. He obviously had something more important to do. The nigga was really starting to get on my nerves, and I didn't like his new attitude. His ass was never around and that shit just didn't sit right with me. Baby Face finally decided to break the ice.

"I'm Baby Face as I'm sure you know, and I'm the oldest. This is my wife Juicy. That's Quick and his wife

Ash, Blaze and his wife Drea, and Kimmie is Shadow's wife he couldn't make it. I gave you the order oldest to youngest. Tell us some shit about you that we don't know. Maybe you can start with the question that was asked the other night. Why didn't you come when our father was supposed to be dead all those years?" You could tell he looked uncomfortable.

"I never knew he was supposed to be dead. Rico was present my entire life. He didn't fake dead with us, so it was no reason to come. This is hard on me as well, I didn't know about you until months ago. My entire life, I thought I was an only child. I'm true to the Hoover blood, I'm the king of my city. I'm here to get to know you. Nothing more, nothing less. I'm single, and I have no kids." The waitress brought our drinks out, and we continued to talk.

"You said he was present in your life, did he live with you and your mom?"

"No, they weren't together. They just messed around from time to time. His relationship was mainly with me. He groomed me to be who I am today." That shit hurt. Our ass grieved his sensitive booty ass, and he was raising another child. Nigga said fuck us, and I was glad we killed him.

"I can't believe that nigga made us think he was dead while he raised another child. Nigga had more secrets than Kimmie's snack bag." Blaze never cut sis a break. He stayed throwing shots.

"How did our father really die?" We all looked at Chuck, then at each other. We weren't keen on telling people our business. Especially people we didn't know.

"We set him on fire, and sent his ass threw a meat chopper. Why you single?" Blaze said that shit like it was nothing, and you could tell our lost brother was pissed. The waitress brought out our food, and it was an eerie silence.

"You sitting here telling me you killed my father and we supposed to eat and crack jokes?"

"Yea nigga, now quit trying to get swoll. Your pants too tight for that shit. This a nice establishment, can't have you around here assed out." Chuck grabbed his gun and stood up. None of us moved. Everyone knew before he could even pull the trigger I would have one in his head. We weren't worried. We all grabbed our forks to eat not paying him any attention when Shadow came busting in the door.

"Blaze put that down. Don't eat that." We all looked at him like he was crazy.

"Nigga I know you be wanting to give your wife all the seconds and shit, but I'm hungry. You can give her the bone to lick when I'm finish." Blaze attempted to eat again, and Shadow knocked it out of his hand.

"Nigga I said don't eat that, I poisoned it." Blaze pulled his gun and pointed it at Shadow. Chuck still had his gun on us and this dinner just got real crazy.

"I'm gone need you to be real clear on what you mean baby brother."

CHAPTER 18 SHADOW

This hitman shit was way more exciting than us robbing banks. It gives you a different kind of rush and I'm able to choose how I want the situation to go. I was happy as hell when G gave me the next hit. This one would show my versatility, and Gangsta will see that I was the right nigga for the job. Looking over the file that was sent to me, I didn't actually know who I was targeting.

It was a way for me to be creative and come up with something different. Since I didn't have anything but his description, I decided to do this one from a distance. The location and time was giving to me, and I headed to the restaurant. Sneaking in the back door to the kitchen, I slid some shit in the food. Paying a waiter, I gave the target's description and told her he would be with a party of people. For five thousand dollars, she better give the shit to the right person. Heading to the building across the street, I grabbed my rifle and looked through the scope to watch it unfold. If the wrong person got the food, I would finish the job from over here.

When I looked through my scope, I noticed my family in there and it hit me. Fuck. When they texted me the details, I didn't really read them because I knew I couldn't make it. Kimmie got the info out of my phone and I didn't think shit else of it. Thinking back on the description, they wanted me to kill Blaze.

Taking off across the street, I ran in and tried to stop Blaze from eating the food. We been at each other a lot lately and he wasn't trying to hear shit I was saying until I announced I poisoned the food.

"I'm gone need you to be real clear on what you mean baby brother." Blaze was pissed, and you could tell he thought I had betrayed him. When I got ready to answer, I noticed our lost brother had his gun raised as well.

"Why the fuck does he have his gun drawn? What the hell is going on?" My ass was lost and I wish I had been at this dinner.

"That's not your concern right now. I need you to explain to us why the fuck you tried to poison Blaze."

Face was even speaking in an aggressive tone, and that wasn't like him.

"Can we talk about this later. I need it to just be us. I will explain everything then." Looking around the room, I could tell that shit wasn't gone fly.

"I don't think you understanding your options. You have about ten seconds before I make Kimmie here a widow. Now what the fuck do you mean you poisoned my food?" Taking a deep breath, I tried my best to explain.

"For the last few months, Gangsta has been training me. I'm a hitman and this was my second job. They never told me who the hit was on and didn't read the text you sent me. All I had was a description. I didn't know I was actually here to kill Blaze. As soon as I put it together, I ran over here to stop it." The look of disappointment covered their faces. In that moment, I realized how I fucked this all up. I should have trusted them enough to tell them and now I felt like shit.

"I think Shadow is right, this is something we need to discuss amongst ourselves. Yall know where to go, Juicy take my keys and drop all the girls off at home. Chuck we will have to take a rain check on this. I'll be in touch." Everyone was protesting to Face's plan.

"You don't run our house, and I need to talk to my husband. His ass needs to come home and figure out if he still has a wife. His brothers can wait." She was right, but my brothers would always come first. Before I could tell her that won't be happening, Blaze went off.

"Listen you big back bitch. This nigga here is our brother. He just tried to kill me and told us he broke code. We need to figure out what the fuck is going on in order to protect his dumb ass. Not to mention, protect you. We have no idea what he is involved in, and that is on us. This don't concern you. He will be home, in the meantime, go swing by Chilis and get you some baby back ribs or some shit."

"Fuck you Blaze, I'm sick of your disrespectful ass." You can see Kimmie was fed up.

"You know you want to. Chilis baby back ribs, I want my Chilis baby back ribs." He actually started singing the song.

"Barbecue sauce." The entire table said the closing line and Kimmie was pissed off. My ass had to intervene.

"This is my wife and if she wants to talk, I will meet you at the house after. You take shit too far, but you gone watch your mouth talking to mine." Blaze fake clutched his pearls and walked up to my face.

"You tough now, nigga we been protecting your bitch ass since you were born. If you hadn't fucked up, we wouldn't even be in this shit. That's just like you though right. Baby brother Shadow, always the fuck up. You trained with G, and now what?" Not backing down, I held my stare.

"Now, I am deadlier than all you niggas. How does it feel to know baby brother can take all of you out in seconds? You mad now because I'm no longer in your Shadow. Well guess what, I don't give a fuck. You have each other, but I'm deadlier."

"We got big dicks though nigga, so you still losing." Everyone fell out laughing including me. This nigga Blaze couldn't be serious to save his life. That's just how we were though, ready to kill each other and then right back laughing. "Now get your ass over to the spot. Kimmie he will be there tonight I promise. Lives are at stake, and we need to know how he fucked up." We all nodded and got up from the table.

Our lost brother was still standing there with malice in his eyes, and I knew we were gone have to watch his ass. Our lives just got flipped upside down, all because I didn't read a fucking text.

Walking Kimmie out to her car, I pulled her to the side. They needed to stay together. Our brother knew we were leaving them alone, and I didn't trust that shit. His ass came out of nowhere and for all I know, he could have been the one to put the hit out on Blaze.

"Don't go to the house. Call the girls and tell them to meet over Quick's house. He has a safe room. Stay there until we come get you. Pay attention to your surroundings, and make sure no one is following you. Tell the girls the same thing. I don't trust this new nigga, and I ain't taking no chances."

"Okay baby, be safe and hurry home." Kissing her, I walked over to my car and headed to the main house. It was about to be a long night.

CHAPTER 19 BLAZE

All kinds of shit were running through my head on the way to the main house. Shadow working with G, and Chuck pulling a gun on us. I know the nigga thought he was doing something, but Quick would have laid his ass out before he could blink. His balls were bigger than my knee caps though. He knew who we were and still upped on us. That took some courage.

Even though I was proud of Shadow for finally being his own man, I was disappointed. We did everything together and that's what made us strong. They knew we were a unit. The only reason someone was trying to step in now, is because they thought we were dismantled. He should have been able to tell us what the fuck was going on.

We all at home retired and bored, and this nigga out there living the life. How the hell he ain't know we wanted to be hitmen too. I've never seen one that uses fire though. My ass would be raw as hell as a hitman.

You could tell the entire car had shit on their mind because no one was talking. It was dead silent in that mother fucker. Even I didn't feel like cracking a joke. I also didn't forget about that tight ass nigga Chuck pulling his gun on us. I couldn't wait to see what the fuck Face was thinking letting that nigga get away.

Ain't no telling what he knew about us, or where we stayed. We pulled up to the house and everybody got out with roaches in they ass. Them mother fuckers were moving out. Taking my time, I walked in the house. Shadow was right behind me. Knowing this wasn't the time to play, I kept my lighter in my pocket. We needed answers and it was only one way to get them.

"The fact that you did something like this and didn't tell us, speaks a lot about your character. You may have trained and got better, but I have lost all respect for you. We are one, and we never make a decision like this without running it by everyone else. If this was something you really wanted to do, we would have let you. Your ass was sneaking for months, for months Shadow. Even after you were done, you said nothing." I've never seen Baby Face this pissed off.

"Do you hear what you said? You would have let me. I'm tired of asking for permission and being treated like a joke. You don't know what it feels like because you never had to go through it." I was sick of Shadow's victim story.

"Cue the fucking violin. All of us except Face has been the baby brother. We all been through it. It wasn't about controlling you, we protected you. We protected each other. You sitting here crying like a bitch in the night, when people would kill to have a circle like ours. You not the only one that gets picked on. I fuck with everybody. You just sensitive as fuck. You wanted to be grown and looked at like a man, and now what? You fucked up. First time out there and you fucked up."

"How did I fuck up Blaze? Because I didn't tell you I was a hitman. Because I poisoned your food that you didn't even eat? How did I fuck up Blaze?" This nigga had no idea.

"This is why we protected you. Your ass don't even have a clue do you? Nigga you fucked up because you didn't complete the hit. You're a hitman right? Or are you a fake one? When you don't complete the hit, the bounty goes on you dumb ass." Just now realizing why everyone was in an uproar, I started panicking.

"Fuck. Fuck. Fuck. I didn't know that. Fuck, I'm sorry yall. Look, I didn't know any of that. G gave me the jobs, and I did them. That's how it went. How was I supposed to know it was on Blaze, and if I didn't do it the hit would go on me?"

"That's our point Shadow. It's a reason why it was all or nothing. We each possess something that the others don't Whether it's quick thinking, reading, shooting, fire, fighting, we're untouchable together. You break that apart then we all are weak. Even though you trained and got better skills, you're still weak without us. Shadow are you not getting this shit? We chose as a group to retire, now your decision has put you and Blaze in jeopardy against someone we don't even know." Face had the nigga damn near in tears.

"Why did he want me dead? I'm confused, I already died it's one of you niggas turn. Why the fuck was he only after me. Especially since we do everything together." The nigga had a dumb look on his face.

"I don't know. The hit was for you only."

"This some bullshit, why the fuck I gotta keep dying. I need to talk to the nigga in charge or something."

"It's not always about you damn. We trying to figure this shit out."

"How the fuck is it not about me when I'm the one that gotta die again?"

"We gone come back tomorrow and try to see what we can do. There is nothing that can be done until we talk to G. He is the one that got the email, and maybe he has the file on who paid for the hit." Face was right, this was pointless.

"I'm not dying again. Just know that."

"Nobody is dying, we just have to figure out what we are up against. It could be our long lost brother. He just happened to show up when the hit is made. It was at the same place we were meeting up with him, and the nigga pulled a gun on us. He obviously cared about Rico and he doesn't like the fact that we killed him.

All of our efforts go into him right now. Somehow it all links back to him. Until we figure out the connection or if it was all him, we will keep him close. Nobody is to be left alone with him and we stay off the grid. Shadow that is for you."

"It's kind of hard to tell a boss like G no. He will kill me."

"Nigga we will kill you. Calm down, we are going to talk to G. There is no way that nigga is going to send you on another hit with a bounty on your head. Kimmie shouldn't be left alone during this shit, and maybe you need to work on fixing your marriage." Quick was on point with that.

"I think we all need to move back into the main house again. It's just safer to have everyone together. This nigga knows where we live, and I'm not feeling that shit at all."

"Blaze if we do this, you have to be cool. Cut Kimmie some slack and control your bad ass daughter." Quick did not like my baby after she burned his hair off.

"I'm just trying not to die again. I ain't got nothing to do with Spark. That's yall niece and yall have to accept her for who she is."

"Alright, move everybody in." Shit was like déjà vu.

CHAPTER 20 GANGASTA

The file didn't tell me that the target was the damn governor. There was no way I could have sent Shadow to do this job. Pulling up to his hotel, I grabbed my bags and got out. Making my way in the hotel, I got on the service elevator. Heading to the roof, I waited on a text. The governor liked young pussy and I hooked him up with just that.

Placing the harness around my waist, I secured it on a pole on the roof. Easing down the side of the building, I looked down and prayed this shit held up. Making my way down three floors, I stopped at the window I needed to be at. Using my glass cutter, I was able to get in the window.

I've done a lot of shit in my life, but a nigga was sweating like a mother fucker. I'm just glad I made it in safe and I prayed I could get back out. I'm sure his security was outside the door, so everything had to be done quietly. Quietly walking through the room, I walked up behind them having sex. Her back was to me and I didn't waste a second. Slicing the governor's throat, in one swift motion, I sliced hers too.

There was no way I could risk her screaming. Heading back to the window, I looked out, and there was no way my ass was going back up that mother fucker. Removing my harness, I walked towards the door and took a deep breath. It was this way, or the window and I wasn't doing that shit again. Pulling both my guns out, I opened the door and started firing.

I knew I had no problem laying they ass out. The hard part would be getting the fuck out of here without getting caught. Running towards the service elevator, I headed downstairs. The police were entering the building from every area, and I knew they were about to lock the building down. Easing out of the side exit, I got the fuck up out of there.

Killing someone in power is not as exciting as the other jobs I have done. The shit had my stress level on ten, and I was paranoid than a mother fucker. Not wanting to waste any more time in this city, I went straight to the airstrip. Getting on the plane, I ordered the pilot to take off immediately. Looking down at my hands, this was the first time my hands ever shook after a hit.

My black ass was so nervous all I could do was laugh. Hanging over the side of a sixteen story building scared me the most. Niggas don't belong on a rubber band. Once we were in the air, I finally started to relax. Laying my head back, I got some much needed rest.

****

When the plane landed, I grabbed my phone and called Shadow. We needed to square up and I had to give him his pay. Not to mention, I wanted to know how he chose to do it. The nigga didn't answer, and I didn't like the feeling that I got from that. Dialing again, I waited, but still no answer.

I needed to make sure Shadow was straight, so I drove to his house. I know I was taking a risk on going to his house and his family finding out, but I had to make sure he was good. When I pulled up, I didn't see his car. Trying the bell anyway, I waited to see if someone would answer. When I didn't get an answer, all I could do was drive home. I would not be the first person to tell his brothers. I'll wait until tomorrow and see if I get a call from him. My gut was telling me shit was all bad, but I tried to be objective. For now, I was gone try to get some sleep.

****

As soon as I woke up, the first thing I did was check my phone. I had a missed call from Face, but I don' t know if he was trying to tell me Shadow was missing. Deciding to take a chance, I called him back.

"Face what's up."

"Get to the main house asap. We'll be there waiting on you."

"On the way." He didn't go into detail, so I guess I wouldn't find out what the fuck was going on until I got there. Knowing I needed a thinker in the room, I called up Suave.

"Bro, we gotta go to the main house. Face needs us something is up."

"What's going on?"

"I don't know. Shadow didn't check in after his hit last night and he wouldn't answer me back. This morning Face called and told me to come to the main house."

"Aight, meet me at my house in twenty." Jumping in the shower, I got my shit together and threw on some clothes.

"Where the fuck are you going negro. You didn't even climb in this pussy last night."

"I was tired, and a lot of shit was on my mind. Something is going on and I need to figure out what it is. Shadow may or may not be missing. Shit just all bad."

"Do what you gotta do but bring your ass back. I need some dick and whether you here or not, I'm getting some." Laughing, I walked out the door. She knew I would beat her ass from the grave. Jumping in my car, I drove to Suave shit to pick him up. As soon as he got in the car, he started in.

"I knew this shit was gone end bad. You couldn't just leave the lil nigga alone. Got him feeling useless and wanted to be trained. Now look what the fuck that happened."

"Nigga, I asked your bitch ass if you thought I should do it, you told me yea. Now it's my fault?" He had a lot of nerve.

"You right, but at the time I hadn't thought about it. Now that something happened, I did. You shouldn't have been fucking with the lil nigga. Got all in his head with that purse dog shit."

"Whatever." It took us about thirty minutes to make it to the main house. The first thing I noticed was Shadow's car. This nigga was ignoring my calls, and now I was pissed. He better had a good explanation. I don't give a fuck if his brothers were mad, this shit is business. Getting out the car, we walked up and rang the bell. Blaze aggy ass opened the door. He wasn't his normal playful self.

"Everybody in here." Me and Suave looked at each other and walked in.

"This might be the first time I ever saw this nigga serious." Suave was right, and I nodded in agreement. All the brothers were there including Shadow. He couldn't look me in the eye, and I wondered if he couldn't go through with the hit and that's why he was scared. Or he fucked the shit up.

"What up yall. Tell him dumb ass." Quick was snapping at Shadow, and now I was intrigued. You could tell Suave was too, because of his face expression.

"I didn't complete the hit last night. It was on Blaze." Looking confused, I thought about the description in my head. It definitely matched that nigga.

"Calm down. I'm not upset with you, because had it been me I wouldn't have done it either. We just have to figure this shit out." This shit just went from complicated to fucked up. My phone beeped, and I knew it was another hit. When I opened up the email, I couldn't do shit but laugh. A bounty was now placed on me and Shadow. Along with the entire Hoover Gang.

"Is it the person that hired me?" Shadow was worried, but he didn't realize how big the shit had just gotten.

"More or less. There is a bounty on your head." Everybody started mumbling, but they didn't know how bad it was. "It is also a bounty on everyone in this room, except for Suave. Shadow not doing the hit automatically puts one on him. I'm the one that hired him, so I guess they put one on me. Your bounty is still open from last night, and I guess they just don't like you niggas."

"How the fuck can you be so calm in the situation? This shit should not be happening. Hell, it would not be happening if it wasn't for dumb ass over here." The real Blaze was starting to show up.

"All we have to do is find out who put the hit out on you in the first place. Right G?" Shadow was getting smarter, but it wouldn't be easy with this one. The client was anonymous.

"So, you supposed to be Shadow of a Gangsta now? Right G. Fuck out of here. I guess you are though, he fucked up and his girl got kidnapped. Now you fuck up and I gotta die again. Both of you niggas some dummies." Just like that, Blaze was back.

"Hold on, don't get your lil ass fucked up." Blaze knew better than to play with me.

"Nigga I ain't scared of you. Fuck you gone do to me? By the time you flick that lil ass knife, u will already be burnt the fuck up. Try me if you want to." Blaze was feeling froggy today. Walking up to Blaze, I was about to reach out and touch this nigga.

"I was just playing." Laughing, I walked off letting him make it. "I'm humbled by your graciousness to forgive me." When I made it across the room, he tried to mumble.

"Punk ass nigga." Looking back at him, he flicked his Bic. Nigga played all his life.

"I'll get my guy to run the IPN the email came from. Until then don't take any more jobs. We have to figure this shit out." Suave finally spoke up. I thought I brought the nigga for nothing he was so quiet.

"We may have a lead. A nigga popped up out of nowhere saying he is our brother. We don't think he lying about that, but he may be pissed because we killed his slip and slide." Fucking with Blaze, I didn't even want to ask. Looking to Face for an explanation, he laughed.

"Our father."

"Like I said, slip and slide. That nigga liked it in the ass. The punk ass nigga pulled a gun on us yesterday when I told him we killed him. He wasn't gone be able to do shit though, his pants were too tight." Blaze started right back in.

"What's his name, I'll have my guy look into him as well."

"Chuck Norris." We all laughed.

"Zavic Hoover." Face must have looked into him as well.

"Do you know where he is staying? Where he is?" Suave was asking all the right questions.

"I'm right here." We all turned to look at the nigga.

CHAPTER 21 ZAVIC

Leaving dinner, I was pissed the fuck off. These niggas just flat out told me they killed my father. I guess when I heard it, I wanted to give them the benefit of the doubt. That was the only reason I came instead of taking they ass out. I'm not a nigga that move off impulse, i wanted to see if what I heard was true.

Learn who they were. Maybe become close. Those niggas don't give a fuck about nobody but they self. They barely give a fuck about each other's wives. The way they went at it, I would have been shot one of they ass. I'm not the hee hee ha ha type and Blaze played entirely too much. All the fuck he did was talk. I don't see how nobody could deal with that shit.

My intentions was not to pull my gun on them, but my anger got the best of me. There was not a hint of sadness in their eyes, and I couldn't let that shit go. The only thing I regret was showing my hand. Now they knew I was a possible enemy and I couldn't have that. It was time I moved different until I figured out how I wanted to handle this shit. My phone rung, and I knew who it was before I even looked.

"What's good."

"You were at the dinner with your brothers, is Blaze dead?" At least I knew who put the hit on him.

"I thought we agreed not to do shit until I talked to them?"

"You did talk to them, and I gave you the chance to hit me up. You didn't so I took it into my own hands.

You think you run this shit, but it was my plan. You wouldn't even know them if it wasn't for me."

"Maybe you should have done your homework. I'm telling you to stand down until I figure this shit out. You about to piss me off, and I promise you don't want to do that. The shit they did to you, will not compare to what I will do. Stand the fuck down." Hanging up the phone, I knew I was gone have to handle him. Even if I allowed the plan to go through with my brothers, I was gone have to take his bitch ass out. Laying down, I knew I was gone have to go talk to these niggas again.

****

Getting up this morning, I jumped in the shower. Even though I was just going to talk to some niggas, I had to get my fly on. Grabbing a Gucci jogging suit, I threw that on with my high top Gucci sneakers. I was tired of Blaze talking about my pants being tight. I've had that same argument with my stylist. She keeps telling me this is the way they dress today, and to keep from looking like a kingpin I had to change my look. I've been buying up a lot of commercial property and trying to find a way to cross over. I wasn't trying to be selling drugs after this year. I've made a lot of money doing what I love, but a nigga was tired of the streets.

When you can walk away on top, then it's a blessing that needs to be taken. I've made it out without ever getting shot, arrested, and no babies. A nigga was winning and I was trying to keep it that way. Grabbing my keys, I headed over to the address I had on file. From what I know, this was the house they held meetings at. I was sure they had to be here. They don't know who is after them, and if it was me, I would pull all my people to a safe house. My mama in a safe house right now, because I had no idea what I was going up against. Pulling up to the address I had, I knew I was in the right spot. Phantoms, Hummers, and a Bugatti was parked out front.

The damn estate was huge. Made my lil mini mansion look like an apartment. I was gone knock on the door, but I decided to go with the element of surprise. You could hear them talking and I decided to stand there and see what I could learn. That Blaze was hell, but he was funny than a mother fucker. They went on about him not doing the hit.

When they admitted to killing our father again, I knew he wasn't just saying the shit to get a rise out of me. They really killed him and didn't have zero fucks to give. A guy I didn't know started asking about me, and I guess it was time to show myself.

"I'm right here." Everyone turned to look at me with shocked expressions on their faces.

"I don't think I like the fact that you keep popping up at our shit. This is one house we don't allow anybody over. How the fuck you get this address?"

"My guy is thorough. I figured we had more to talk about. Seeing the mural on the wall of Blaze, it made me think about the death certificate I had of him. "What's that all about?"

"I like looking at myself. What the fuck do you want? You mad about your bitch ass father? Why are you here?" He was on point, but I wasn't going to tell them that.

"I'm just trying to figure out what happened. I had nothing to do with a hit being put out on you. All I want is answers." Since I didn't know about the hit, I didn't lie.

"Nigga we gave you the answer. You think because you bought bigger pants, we would see you differently? Now you just a loose bitch. You know my wife?" Laughing, I tried my best to keep my temper in check.

"I want to know why you killed him?" I could see the guy I didn't know staring at me, and it made me feel eerie. Like he was reading me inside out.

"Does it matter? I'll tell you why we killed him if you tell us why it matters. Let's say we killed him because we wanted his money. Will that upset you and push you to retaliate? Or if we say he was a rapist, will it be all good then? Honestly, does it matter why we killed him? You here to avenge him right? Anything we tell you will it really make it okay in your eyes?" Thinking it over, I really didn't know the answer to Face's question.

"I don't know. It matters because he was my father. He raised me, groomed me, taught me how to be a man. Yes, I would want to avenge him. Is there a good enough reason that will make me say fuck it, I don't know. Right now, all I am looking for is answers." The guy that was staring me down made me feel like I needed to answer honestly. It's like he would know if I was lying.

"That's real enough. I guess we owe you an explanation." Before Face could finish his sentence, shots rang out. I never had time to grab my gun before I was hit. My body jerked every way possible. I was on fire, and I knew there was no way I would make it out of here alive. Looking up at my brothers, they were shooting at the assailant. Once the gun shots stopped, I was already coughing up blood.

"Grab him now, we have to take him to the hospital. Hurry the fuck up." That was the last thing I heard before my eyes closed.

CHAPTER 22 BABY FACE

"Why the fuck we saving this nigga, he might be here to kill us. I don't trust his stylish ass. Anybody that dress better than me don't need to be in my city. I have a complex about that shit."

"Shut up Blaze." Everybody shouted at the same time. Picking him up, we carried him to my truck. Jumping inside, I knew we needed somebody to stay behind. Even though G was indirectly involved, this was an issue concerning my brothers. They could stay there and protect our family.

"Suave, can yall stay here with the girls to make sure nobody comes back? We can't leave them here without protection."

"You don't even have to ask. We got you. One thing for certain, it's always good to have Lucifer on your side."

"If you don't have enough ammo, go upstairs to any of the rooms. It's a safe in each one and the codes are the same. It's the old building number. You know which one. Just so you know, I have never in life given someone outside of my brothers that code, so you know I trust you with my life. Air anybody out that comes within five hundred feet of that house."

"Five hundred feet? You do know that means a car driving by right?" Shooting Blaze a look, he threw his hands up and sat back. Driving off, I went as fast as I could to get him to the hospital. Even though I didn't know his intentions, whoever was shooting was aiming for him. No one was paying attention and he was the only one that got hit. That tells me it's someone else in the picture, and they didn't want him here with us. That said a lot.

"Face, are you sure we are doing the right thing? I know how we are about each other, but is he one of us? We could be saving him to take us out in the end." Quick was right, but my gut was telling me to save him.

"I'm telling you bitches now, I'm not dying again. It's one of yall turn." I think Blaze being the target was really bothering him.

"At the end of the day, he is our brother. No matter how fucked up our father was. He is a Hoover and until he shows us different, we will treat him as one." Everyone got silent, and I knew it bothered them to help save someone we didn't know. Pulling up to the hospital, we grabbed him and rushed him inside.

"Can we get some help?" The nurses saw all the blood and they all rushed over.

"What's his name?"

"Zavic Hoover."

"Okay Zavic stay with us. We are going to take care of you. Get operating room four ready. We have a multiple gunshot wound, with a very low pulse." They wheeled him off and it was starting to feel like déjà vu.

"Why yall didn't drive me to the hospital? If yall did, I wouldn't have died and shit. I can say one thing, sitting here waiting to find out the results is fucking with me." I knew that feeling too well.

"We were at a public place and the people called the ambulance. You know I wouldn't have let that go down if I could have stopped it bro. You here now and you not going nowhere." Realizing Shadow hadn't said a word, I knew what was going on. I saw that same guilt with Quick. "Baby bro, it's not your fault. If you hadn't taken the hit someone else would have and they would have killed Blaze."

"It has to be personal. It's like they wanted him to be killed by one of his own. They knew me or G would do the hit. They didn't include his name or anything. Just location and description. We need to figure out who is out there that we fucked over and we will find the person." Thinking about it, that shit made perfect sense. It was only one problem though.

"Blaze has pissed off everyone at one point or another, so that's hard. The Hoovers as a whole, we got rid of all our enemies."

"Did we? Anybody we take out, they have family or friends. Just like Chuck in there. If we kill him, we don't know who will come after us on his behalf. It could be anyone. Chuck is our only hope at who this is after us." Quick was on point as well.

"Well then they better save Chuck. We need that nigga. If he dies though, I get his pants." Everybody laughed because Blaze been giving that nigga shit since we met him. Now he wants the damn pants. I hated that we had no idea what was waiting for us. The fate of the Hoovers was in the wind for the first time in our lives.

****

We had been waiting for six hours, and the doctors finally came out to talk to us. My ass was tired and hungry. Standing to figure out what happened, the doctor approached us.

"His surgery was good, and we successfully removed all the bullets. He's in recovery right now, but he will be okay. We sedated him for the time being, other than that he is fine." I don't know why, but I felt relieved.

"Thank you doctor. Can we go see him?"

"Yes, room 652." We all walked to the back, and he didn't look like he was just lit up. I'm happy that he made it out, but it was weird. This nigga had to be hit at least ten times, and he is fine. My ass was hit a couple of times and the shit was touch and go.

"Me and Shadow gone ride back to the house to update the others and check on things. You two stay here. Someone needs to protect him just in case they come for him. If he wakes up, call me." You could tell Blaze wanted to protest, but I walked off before he could. If they knew the real reason I was leaving, they would be pissed. I needed some pussy just in case shit went bad. I was stressed, and pussy always made me think better.

"You really believe this isn't my fault?" As soon as we got in the car, Shadow started that guilt trip shit.

"Maybe it is, but we all fucked up at one point or another. I meant what I said. We just have to figure it out like we always do. Beating up on yourself ain't gone make it better. Nigga I thought you were trained by

Lucifer. Don't you supposed to be without feelings and shit?" He laughed and nodded.

"Yea, but I don't have that shit all the way down pact. I'm getting there."

"Do you like what you are doing? You happy with yourself now?" You could see him thinking.

"Yeah I am, but not at the expense of my brothers. I didn't mean for this shit to happen, but I won't stop until I figure the shit out." Nodding, I didn't respond. I knew he was gone have to figure this shit out on his own. We could no longer keep him under our wing. Baby brother wanted to fly.

When we got to the house, I ran inside to make sure everything was good. Suave and G were sitting there with the girls and everything was okay.

"Juicy upstairs now." She knew the look and jumped up.

"Blaze gone beat your ass when he found out you came home to get some pussy and didn't let him get none." Laughing at Gangsta, I ran up the stairs. As soon as I walked in, I freed Tsunami. His ass didn't even flop down. He was on brick and Juicy had him in her mouth before I could say a word.

She was sucking the fuck out my dick and I was turned on like a mother fucker. Knowing I didn't have that much time, I pulled her head back. Bending down, I grabbed her legs and flipped her into a hand stand.

"The blood gone rush to the top of my head. I'm not gone be able to breathe baby."

"This nut about to be fast. By the time the blood gets to the top, my nut gone be mixed with it. Now shut the fuck up and take this mother fucker." Pushing my dick in, I used her legs to pull her back and forth against my dick. Juicy was scared of this position, but the shit felt good as fuck. It's like my dick was in her throat.

When she started throwing it back, I knew I wasn't gone last long. Getting good grip, I slammed into her juicy ass pussy. Even though I was about to nut fast, I refused to let her win. Sticking my finger in her ass, I fucked her in both holes as my nut rose up.

"Catch this nut baby. I'm cumming." Picking up the pace, I allowed my seeds to cover her walls. Once I was done shaking, I dropped her, and she hit her head.

"Why the fuck would you do that asshole?"

"I gotta hurry up and get back before Blaze realize what I did. Plus, him and Zavic don't get along. If he wakes up, they ass might have a shootout in that bitch."

"Yeah, you better hurry the fuck up. You know how that nigga is." Doing a quick wash over my dick, I headed downstairs.

"Shadow let's go. Suave let me know if you hear something from your guy."

"I got you, go check on your brother." That shit seemed weird. We got another brother.

CHAPTER 23 BLAZE

Fuck what them doctors talking about, this nigga looked like he was on his last leg. Walking over to his belongings, I pulled his clothes out. I was checking them out when Quick stopped me.

“Nigga what the fuck are you doing?”

“I’m trying to see if the nigga my size. If he dies, I’m going to find where he staying at. Nigga gone be fly as shit.” Me and Quick fell out laughing.

“I thought my pants were too tight. The fuck you want my clothes for?” We looked over at the bed, and Chuck was awake.

"Nigga don't nobody want your clothes. I was trying to see how many times they shot your flawed ass. They lit your ass up too."

"It's all good, I know the truth. Where everybody at, I need to talk to you all about something."

"Talk then nigga." His ass was trying to be dramatic and shit. "You acting like you about to die."

"You don't seem like the serious one, so I will wait until Face is here. You play too damn much, and I'll be done killed your bitch ass."

"True, but not about you killing me though. You may as well get that shit out your mind, you can't fuck with us. If it had been us, you would be somewhere turning to ashes." We both laughed.

"That's kind of what I want to talk to yall about. Can you call Face?"

"I'm here, what's up?" Face and Shadow walked back in and I was glad, I hated waiting on people to tell me something. My ass needed to know right then.

"I know who is after you." Now we were back looking at him like the disloyal fool ass bitch made punk we thought he was. Nigga had me doing my Denzel look and all. "Two months ago, it was an envelope on my porch and it contained a bunch of information on The Hoover Gang. All the banks you robbed and people you killed. It's like someone was keeping a file on you.

I had no idea how it pertained to me, but I assumed we were related because of the last name. Not knowing what they wanted me to do with the information, I waited. A couple of days passed, and he showed up at my door. He told me that you all were my brothers and you killed our father for his money. I wasn't sure if it was true or not, so I did my own investigation. You were the last people he was seen with, so I decided to come here to find out what happened. The plan was to avenge his death if you were behind it." You could hear me pissing in a bitch's ear it was so quiet.

"He wanted me to kill you all off GP and got mad when I wouldn't do it, and I guess that's why he came after me." We all sat there quiet, until I broke the ice.

"Nigga you acting like Face and shit. You just said all that and we still don't know who the fuck HE is."

"HE is Officer Tate." What the fuck.

"That's impossible. We killed that nigga. Hell, I lit that nigga up like the fourth of July and Shadow put a bullet in him." The look he gave me made it make sense. "That's why the hit was on me, and he wanted Shadow to do it." Chuck nodded, and I was pissed off.

"Wait. I'm trying to think about that day. You set him on fire, and Shadow shot him. We walked out, and you set the house on fire. He must not have died. Fuck. Shadow your ass can't shoot for shit." Face was trying to put it together.

"You telling me some baked ass crunch cake is mad at me for some fucked up shit he did? He lucky he lived."

"You fucked him up. The nigga not even recognizable. Now that I told you all this, it's time for a moment of truth. Why did you kill our father?" Knowing I wasn't the right person to explain this shit, I let them niggas take the lead.

"Him and Tate was fucking my girl getting info on us, and they were fucking each other. He had Blaze shot up at my wedding and then switched the bodies. The nigga had us thinking our brother was dead. Nigga started back fucking our mama taking all her money, but he was fucking Tate. My mama found out and he damn near beat her to death. He owed a lot of money to a Cartel and he was back to get the money from us. We thought he was dead all those years. Blaze told him he would never get a dime and that's why he tried to kill him." You could tell that was a lot for that nigga to take in. He thought it was gone be some simple ass dumb shit. I don't give a fuck how mad that nigga is, if Rico walked in the door now, I would kill him again.

"I understand why you did it and that nigga don't need to be avenged. Know I was coming here for facts, and if it was worth me avenging, I would have." I was starting to like Chuck, he was a cocky nigga.

"Now what do we do?" I wanted to know the plan, fuck all this holding hands and singing nursery rhymes ass bullshit.

"We go after that nigga and put him down once and for all. I'll have my people looking for him, and you get your people. We will find that nigga, and when we do we gone finally put that fire out." We all gave each other the look of approval.

"What's your skill? Each of us are a beast at something. You're one of us, so what is it?" Shadow must have been scared he was gone outshine the shit he just learned, but I was curious too, so I shut up.

"I'm raw with guns, but I'm a beast with a knife. I like that up close and personal shit. The feeling of flesh tearing under my hand, man that's a feeling like no other." We looked at this nigga like he was crazy.

"You sure you not related to Gangsta instead of us? We from the same hood, was your mama a hoe? I'm just asking."

"Nigga talk about my mama again imma beat your ass. Ain't nobody say shit about that damn shag rug your mama had on her head." Oh yeah, he was gone fit right in.

"God, how the fuck we get two niggas just the same. You act just like Blaze." We all laughed at Shadow.

"I'm telling my mama too Chuck. Just so you know. I'm the only one that talk about my mama shit."

"Can yall start calling me Vic now damn. Yall say that shit like it's really my name." I guess he ain't like Chuck.

"I was Purse Dog for a long time thanks to Gangsta. Once someone calls you something, it sorta just sticks."

"Yall keep saying Gangsta, are you referring to the one and only. You know Lucifer?" Everybody knew that nigga.

"Yea, he was at the house earlier. Him and his brother Suave."

"Them niggas are legends in Kentucky. They say he eat people, is that true?"

"We don't know, but we heard that too. Only thing I can tell you is that nigga sick as hell. Don't ever cross him." We all agreed with Face.

"Now what we gone do with this burnt ass nigga Tate?"

CHAPTER 24 TATE

These niggas had me fucked up if they thought shit was that easy. They tried to kill me like I was a nigga on the street. I'm a fucking officer, well not anymore but at the time I was. They killed my bitch, then killed Rico and that nigga was the love of my life. Nobody has ever fucked me like that nigga.

Now who the fuck was gone want me. The only thing you could see on my face is my eyes. Blaze was going to feel the same shit I go through every day. At first, I wanted Shadow to take out his own brother. That shit would have cut them deep, but now, I wanted that nigga to suffer.

He was out there living his life like he didn't fuck over a lot of people. That bitch ass nigga was about to die for real this time. In a slow painful way. I may even get ten niggas to tear a lining out his ass.

Nigga walk around life thinking everything funny, but I would get the last laugh. That was the worse day of my life, and I will never forget it. That nigga set me on fire from the inside out. The doctors were shocked that I made it. The bullet wound didn't do any damage.

Most of my damage came from the fire. Shadow's bitch ass couldn't shoot to save his life, but that Blaze was deadly with that fire. After extensive rehab, and them trying skin grafts, I was finally released. The first thing I did was dig into their lives. Looking for an opening, but I found none. I started looking into Rico hoping I could find someone in his past that would want to avenge his death, I ran across some info on Zavic. Before I approached him, I wanted to research who I was dealing with and his relationship with Rico. It was just my luck when Shadow's name started ringing bells out here in the streets. Finding out he was a hitman, I put my plan into motion.

Zavic wasn't like his other brothers. He was soft. Nigga wanted to come here and talk. I knew I needed to light a fire under his ass, so I put the hit out on Blaze. I figured they would blame him, and both of my problems would die at the same time.

The shit didn't work out like that and I had to improvise. If Zavic thought I was going to let him turn on me, he had another thing coming. After our phone call, something told me to follow his ass. Just like the bitch I thought he was, he headed straight to them. The fact that they were in there talking and they hadn't killed him, I knew he was ratting me out. I wanted another day for The Hoover brothers, so I aimed solely at him.

I didn't have a crew, but I didn't need one. I had pure hate pushing me, and I refused to stop until Blaze got everything he had coming to him. This was more than payback, this was war.

CHAPTER 25 SHADOW

Since our brother was good, and it seemed we were accepting him into the family, I needed to head back to the house. Me and Kimmie still hadn't had a chance to talk, and I needed to make sure she was good.

"Hey yall, imma head to the house and check on Kimmie. We haven't talked since all of this started, and I may not have a damn wife to go home to if I don't fix this shit."

"Nigga she about to eat your ass up. Might as well call your ass Shadow biscuit." Blaze got on my nerves, but I couldn't do shit but laugh.

"Fuck you nigga. You the reason she gone divorce my ass. Let me get up out of here. I'll be back up in here in a couple of hours to check on you Vic. I'll Update G and them on what's going on."

"Aight, we will be by later. It always has to be somebody here, so we will take turns. Blaze you can go with Shadow and get you a break. Next, Quick can go." Nodding at Face, I got ready to walk out the room.

"Yall steady underestimating a nigga. You better do your homework on me. I'm good. Yall niggas go be with your families and come back up here tomorrow." You could tell he was used to being by his self.

"Nigga don't nobody care how good you are. That's not how we get down. We done had the deadliest niggas laying where you are, and we don't leave them alone. Until you walk out these doors, someone will be here with you. If you want us home with our families, then you need to hurry up and heal. You got family now, get used to it." Quick didn't like the nigga at first, but I see everyone was coming around. I was shocked at Blaze, he usually don't like nobody.

"Come on nigga, so we can get back up here."

"I'm coming mother fucker damn." Walking out, we got in the truck and drove to the main house. My ass was tired, and barely had any sleep. I wish I could take a nap, but I needed to make shit right with my girl. Blaze fell asleep as soon as we got in the car. When we pulled up, I hit the nigga letting him know we had made it.

Climbing out the car, we headed inside. Blaze bitch ass went straight upstairs. Nigga didn't even try to come talk to they ass with me. They were in the front discussing our problem.

"We know who behind the shit. It was the officer we killed in all the bullshit with our father. The nigga didn't die, and he holding a grudge because Blaze burned him so bad you can't recognize the nigga. His ass shot up Zavic as well."

"Okay, now we working with something. My guy can find anybody. I'll call him and get him right on it. We gone bring our families over before our ass be divorced. We also need someone here to stay with the women once we go after the nigga. Just in case he got a crew behind him." Suave ass was on it.

"That's fine. Face said we have to stay at the hospital until Vic gets out. No need in staying away from your families."

"Aight bet, while you here, we gone swing by and go get them. Be back in a minute." Suave and G left and I headed upstairs. Kimmie was laying in the bed looking so beautiful. This woman had a nigga heart and I needed to make sure she knew it. Climbing in the bed with her, I wrapped my arms around her belly.

"Hey baby, is everything ok?"

"Not yet, but it will be. We know who behind it, and we are going to handle it. Right now, I don't want to talk about that. We need to talk baby. I know I've been fucking up but know I have not been with another woman. It was something I needed to do for me.

Everybody always treated me like I was scared of them or allowing them to run over me. It's just how we are with each other. It's how we always been. I started feeling insecure about myself and my own abilities. To be the man you needed me to be, I had to do it. G had rules, and I couldn't break them if I wanted him to train me. Telling you or my brothers was forbidden and turning off my feelings for you was mandatory. You never have to worry about another bitch taking your place. I need you. Do you understand that?"

"I don't give a fuck what he told you. I'm your wife, you could have written a bitch a note or something telling me to keep quiet. I wouldn't have said a word, but you have to have faith in me as well. Let me support you and back everything you want to do. Let me be your wife. Don't shut me out like that again or I will leave your ass."

"Girl you ain't going nowhere. I feed you too much good food." When she slapped me, I grabbed her to me and kissed her with so much passion. I hated that I kept it from her. What worked for G was fine, his family is different. Me and mine could have dealt with this differently. I would never keep anything else like this from them. That's not what we do.

Rubbing my hand up her legs, I was happy to find her with no panties on. Rubbing against her clit, her shit was soaking wet. Needing to taste it, I went down and licked every last drop. After she came in my mouth twice, I got up ready to make love to my wife. Bending over, she took me in her mouth. I loved the way she gave me head, and I was in heaven until she screamed.

"Baby what's wrong."

"Your crooked ass dick must have hit my cervix. I'm in labor. Fuuuckkkk. Come on baby we gotta go."

"Girl my dick ain't even that big, how it reach your cervix? You sure you in labor?" When she squeezed my hand, I knew she was sure. It felt like she broke my shit. My dumb ass started screaming all through the house trying to get everybody up. Running in the hallway, they looked at me like I was crazy.

"Kimmie in labor. We gotta get to the hospital." Everybody took off to go get dressed. Carrying her to the car, I started to think it was a bad idea. I damn near dropped her four times. Not waiting on the others, I left and drove fast as hell. She was in so much pain it was scaring me. This was my first baby and I didn't know how this shit went.

When we pulled up to the hospital, I was smart. I ran in and got a wheel chair. There was no way I was picking her ass up again. Pushing her inside, I told them what was going on and they took us to labor and delivery. My ass was so nervous, I almost forgot to call Face. Grabbing my phone, I dialed his number while they prepped Kimmie.

"Brother we upstairs in room 819. Kimmie is in labor. Everybody on their way here, so we should be good. They prepping her now, so hurry up."

"Aight, we on our way up there." Hanging up, I continued to rub my wife's hair. She was in so much pain, I wish I could take it away from her.

The doctors instructed her to push, and I went to the foot of the bed to watch the birth of my first child.

That head started pushing that pussy loose, I tried to walk away, and I passed the fuck out.

When I woke up, Kimmie was holding the baby. How the fuck I miss the birth of our first child. All the shit I have done over these past few months, who would have ever thought a big pussy would be the thing to take me out.

"Damn yall could have woke me up. Let me see." Grabbing the baby, tears fell from my eyes as I stared into the eyes of my son.

"Do you all have a name?"

"Zavien Hoover, Jr." Looking over at Kimmie, I never loved anyone as much as I loved her in that moment. After I spent some time with him all by myself. I gave him over to Kimmie, so I could go get the others.

The entire Hoover family was in the waiting room, and I wouldn't trade my family for shit in the world. We had our flaws, but we stood by each other no matter what. Knowing we shouldn't have that many visitors, we all headed back to the room. When we walked in, Kimmie was in the bed but the baby was gone.

"Damn brother, your girl done ate the baby. I told yall we should have stopped and got her some Popeyes." Too happy to be upset with Blaze, I couldn't do shit but laugh. I was surprised Kimmie laughed as well.

"They took the baby to run tests. He will be back in a few minutes. Everyone talked shit and waited for the nurses. When she walked in, you could tell she was scared as hell to see this many niggas in one spot. All the shit that Blaze talks, he was the first one to grab the baby.

"Hey nephew, it's uncle Blaze. You gone hang out with me and Spark all the time. Zavi don't fuck with us like that. You want a lighter, huh you want a lighter." Face took the baby from his psycho ass, and they continued to pass the baby around. In this moment, we weren't worried about anything or anybody. Right now, shit was just perfect.

"I'm starting to think we gotta watch this nigga Quick. Spark came out looking just like him, and now this lil nigga look like him too." Grabbing the baby, I looked at him and Blaze wasn't lying. Everybody looked at Quick as if he had some explaining to do.

"Nigga please. I like baked chicken wings. Your girl a big ass fried breast. No offense." Sticking up my middle finger at him, I walked back over to Kimmie and gave her the baby.

Grabbing my phone, I took a lot of pics. This was a special moment and with Tate on the loose, we didn't know if everybody would make it out safely. For now, we were all together, and I wanted to capture it all.

CHAPTER 26 GANGSTA

It's been so much going on, we hadn't had time to get at Tate. The birth of the baby and Vic having to heal, shit had to be put on hold. Now that everything was in order, we were ready to roll. Our guy got back to us, and someone else put a hit out on me. It wasn't personal, just business. I was Shadow's boss, and the bounty had to be put on my head for hiring him and he botched the job. They didn't give a fuck that it was his brother.

I could let the shit ride, but I don't like the idea of someone wanting me dead still walking around living. After we were done with Tate, we were swinging by to pay that nigga a visit as well. This time, no enemy will be left standing. This was the end and we wanted to make sure we did it right. Everyone was saying their goodbyes, but I was arguing with my wife.

"Why the fuck me and Tank gotta stay here with they ass. Them our bitches and all, but these hoes ain't gone shoot piss on a nigga. You know I like to be in the action, why the fuck I can't go?" Me and Suave went through the most trying to keep our girls in check. I'm sure his ass was having the same argument.

"Baby, it's only two mother fuckers and it's already seven of us. We don't need no extra hands. We didn't even call Smalls, so you know it ain't that serious. We not going to war, just tying up loose ends. Just in case we underestimated this nigga, we need you to be here. If a nigga come here, you already said they can't protect shit. Now quit pouting and go get your daughter. Hurry the fuck up."

"Hey man, yall baby over here shitting on my picture. I'm about to drop kick her shitty ass. G, what kind of nasty ass demon you raising?" I laughed because I tried to tell Paradise before they saw her. You couldn't take Kenya's ass nowhere.

"It's just her thing. We don't know why she do that shit. I'll have my homie paint you a new one." This nigga was actually pissed. The nigga alive and well, but mad over a memorial picture.

"Nigga I died. Do you hear me, I died. Your daughter just gone shit all on my grave like I ain't shit. She gotta stay on the porch until we get back. Loosey, if she shits anywhere else, show Spark where my lighters at. Let her light her booty hole on fire." This nigga was doing the most. Signaling for the fellas to come on, I eased out while Paradise was cleaning up shit. We all jumped in two cars and headed to the house where Tate was staying.

"Is he always this extra?" Vic was asking about Blaze and I knew the feeling, but I been dealing with the shit since we were kids.

"You have no idea. This is actually him calm. His ass is maturing, but you did not want to know this nigga two years ago." Suave shook his head in agreeance. All of us had grown, and that's why this shit needed to end. When we pulled up, we parked down the street, so we wouldn't alert him of our presence.

Crouching down, we made our way to the back door. Not even trying to play around, I kicked the door open. This nigga jumped up and tried to take off running. Before I could do anything, a knife went flying past my face. Everybody turned around, and looked at Vic. Looking back at Tate, the knife was through his eye holding him against the wall.

“Well shit, I guess that is your thing.” Blaze was in awe of this nigga. I ain’t gone lie, I was too. Now wanting to see if it was just a fluke, I wanted to see the shit again.

“Vic, can you do that shit twice?”

“With my eyes closed.” My ass was impressed.

“Ten racks say you can’t. Fuck that. You not about to out dress us and be Jackie Chan in this bitch. We said you Chuck Norris now your ass trying to switch the shit up. Your thing is tight pants." Everybody fell the fuck out, but Vic took Blazes bet. We found a towel and tore it down the middle. Tying it over Vic's eyes, I spent him around until he had no clue which way he was facing. The nigga was facing me, and I prayed he didn't soar a knife my way. I would hate to kill they brother and they just met his ass. This nigga gripped the knife and took a breath. He was still facing me, and I was starting to get nervous.

In one swift motion, he turned towards Tate and threw the knife in his other eye. That nigga threw that shit so hard the wind shifted my eyebrows. Tate ass must have passed out or died from the first knife because the nigga didn't make a sound.

"Nigga, that shit is impressive as fuck." Untying the towel, he smiled at his work. Shrugging his shoulders, he acted as if it was nothing. That let me know his ass had more tricks up his sleeve.

"It was alright." Blaze was mad he had to give up that money. Walking over to Tate, the nigga was trying to play dead. "Damn nigga you ugly as shit. Looking like a baby Freddy Krueger. One two the Hoovers are coming for you. Three four you nailed to the door." This nigga Blaze didn't know when to quit.

"We fucked up the last time, but we won't make the same mistake again." Shadow wanted to show off his new skills and turned his back to Tate. Pointing his gun under his arm, he shot Tate in the head six times. His brothers were looking at him shocked.

"I hope you don't mind me not taking any more chances." Grabbing my machete, I took his head off in one motion. "Let's get the fuck out of here before the cops come. I bet that nigga don't come back no more. Vic, get your knives out of his shit." The nigga didn't look disgusted or nothing. Yeah, his ass a beast.

****

We were sitting outside the nigga Don's house, trying to analyze the situation. Tired of waiting, I got out the car and headed towards the door. When they saw I was going in, they jumped out as well. Trying the knob, it was unlocked, and we walked in. A bullet flew by my face and almost took me out. Guess the nigga knew we were coming.

The war began. Everyone started shooting. I wasn't worried because me and Quick could lay down an army by ourselves. Bodies were dropping, and Suave was the one laying most of them out. Guess the nigga really missed this shit. The last guy standing was running and shooting in our direction. Shadow came out of nowhere and took his entire back off with his shot gun.

Looking at the bodies on the ground, I didn't see Don. We walked through the house, but we didn't find him. This nigga was nowhere to be found.

"Hey, it's a basement over here." Grabbing our guns, we headed downstairs. The nigga had his ass hiding while his crew was up there getting lit up. I didn't like bitch shit like that.

"Didn't you know you can't kill Lucifer?" The guy looked scared out of his mind, but I didn't give a fuck. Walking over to him, slammed him to the ground. Pushing my knee in his chest, I took my knife to his eye. Suave walked over and held him down. The guy was screaming and fighting for dear life. Tired of the shit, Suave bashed his face in with his gun until he was knocked out. Looking around the room, I smiled at the fellas.

"One last time?" Face and Blaze threw they hands up telling us to do our thang. They wanted no parts of this shit. Me, Suave, and Shadow started cutting the nigga body up. It was no reason too, but we had to go out with a bang since it was our last hurrah.

"Yall niggas doing that shit messy as fuck. Hold on." This nigga Vic tossed his knife at Don's wrist and tore that mother fucker clean off. He had to have some kind of special blades. How the fuck was he breaking through the bones like that? Doing it a few more times, he made the shit easy as hell for us. After we were done, we were walking out.

"Blaze, you not gone do your thang?" He was about to flick his Bic when Shadow did a trick with his lighter and flung it at Don's remains. It looked like the nigga threw a fireball.

"Who the fuck you think you are? That nigga off Mortal Kombat. Finish him looking ass. What's his name?" You could tell Blaze was mad Shadow took his thing.

"His name is Blaze." Face was trying to hold in his laugh.

"Oh hell naw nigga you got me fucked up. It's only one Blaze you better go eat people with Gangsta."

"Nigga I don't eat shit but pussy and food, you got me fucked up." I wonder where the hell that rumor came from. Blaze stepped forward and raised his hands.

"Technically, if you a cannibal a person is considered food. I'm just saying."

"Shut up Blaze." Everybody yelled at his aggy ass.

"I'm sorry. Please don't eat me." When I cut my eyes at him, he flicked his Bic. Laughing, I went to walk out of the basement.

"THE DAY OF THE GEECHIE IS OVER. NAW FUCK THAT, I'm not gone keep being scared. I'm about to burn the souls he ate out his asshole." Turning around, I knocked the lighter out his hand. "I'm sorry I was just playing." We all laughed as Blaze set the basement on fire. Even though Shadow learned a few tricks, everyone knew nobody did fire like Blaze.

Easing out the back door, we all headed to the car. When I looked back, I didn't see Blaze.

"Where that nigga at?" We stopped walking and looked towards the house. He came running out when we heard the explosion.

"Nigga wasn't about to show me up with my shit. Now the nigga wanna throw fire. I'll flick my Bic on your eyelid pussy ass nigga. Let's go." Jumping in the car, we let Blaze have his rant. The shit was finally over.

CHAPTER 27 BLAZE

A nigga was pissed all the way back to the house. My own brother trying to snake me out of my shit. Nigga could have learned to slap a bitch with some water. Why the fuck he wanna learn my shit. I had to leave out doing my thing. Nobody, and I mean nobody can make a bomb out of a lighter, but I can. This nigga in there flicking fire like spit balls and shit.

Then Vic ass in there throwing knives and shit, like a damn Chinese midget. I think me, Face, and Quick was getting old. I'm glad we were retired or we were gone have to learn some new shit. They ass got us looking like the weak links of the group. I got a trick for they ass though. My ass was getting old, but I knew somebody that wasn't. Pulling up at the house, everybody had questions because we were covered in blood. Mainly Suave, Shadow, and G since they were down there cutting up bodies and shit.

We all headed upstairs to shower before we explained anything. After we washed our ass, we headed downstairs and I was happy as hell my mama cooked. She was standing there pissed that we brought Vic to the main house.

"Ma, this is Vic. Our brother. I know what your punk ass husband did, but he has nothing to do with that. You gone have to accept him like we did." Face tried to talk some sense into her ass.

"I ain't gotta accept nobody. How you aint know if I wanted to fuck his ass? Bringing the nigga in here talking about a damn step son. He can step off in this tiger though. Come here baby come taste mama's greens." Vic was looking shocked, but he had no idea this was calm for her.

"Ma, if you don't go sit your ass down somewhere looking like Don Cheadle. Wig on side lean and you trying to talk to somebody. Madea family reunion wig having ass." I'm sick of her ass.

"Fuck you bitch. Just gone stand there and disrespect your mama. Who raised your ass? Get yall dusty asses in here and eat. I should fart in the damn pot. Always talking shit."

"Bro that's how you talk to your mama?" Everybody laughed at Vic question.

"They been arguing like that since that nigga was a kid. That's her favorite child. He can't do no wrong in her eyes." Face was talking shit, but everybody knew it was the truth. All I could do was smile. I loved the shit out of my mama. We went in the family room and ate. Once we were done, I grabbed Spark and whispered in her ear. Sliding her my lighter, I let her down off my lap.

Drea was looking at me big eyed because she knew I had her up to something. Shrugging my shoulders, I laughed as I waited on the aftermath. It was only a matter of time before it kicked off.

"Who the fuck daughter is this." Everybody ran in the front as Vic jumped up screaming. Spark tried to run to me, but Vic tripped her ass.

"Why would you do that to a kid. God is not pleased." Trying to hold in my laugh, I held my serious face.

"That lil girl burned off my fucking beard. Who is she?" Everybody looked over to me. "I should have known she was your damn child. I'm about to fuck you up." I flicked my Bic and tried to back out the room, and this nigga threw a knife at my ass. My arm and the lighter was pinned to the wall by my shirt.

"Nigga you could have took my hand off. My daughter did not mean to make you look like pedophile Sam. She doesn't know you. It's not even that bad. Loosey, go draw him a beard on right quick." Snatching his knife out my shirt, he started laughing.

"You aggy as fuck bruh. Did you get it out your system? Try me again your ass gone be using your toes to flick that Bic." Not scared of nobody, when he walked off, I got the edge of his hairline. Taking off running, my ass almost made it to the stairs until my funky ass child tripped me.

"Tripping game daddy. I win."

"I swear I hate your snitching traitor ass. Go to bed." The entire house laughed as I laid on my back stuck. I'm glad Vic wasn't on no bullshit because a nigga couldn't get up if I tried. Drea came to help me up. As we went up the stairs, I got pissed again.

"I want a DNA test. Ain't no way that baby mine. She ain't shit."

"Hey bro, I'm about to head to the hotel. I got an early flight tomorrow." Turning around, I yelled down the stairs.

"There is no way we letting you leave without blessing you in and we got our own plane you commercial ass bitch." Technically it was G's plane, but so what. We can use that bitch when we want to.

****

Everybody was getting dressed, and a fly nigga like me was ready. Wearing a Gucci cashmere sweater, some jeans, and my Gucci gym shoes. I threw on my Movado to finish off my look. Brushing my waves down, I sprayed on my cologne and I was ready.

"Baby, can the girls come today?" Looking at Drea like she lost her mind, I licked my lips to emphasize how good I was looking.

"You tried it. It's a brother thing, yall already know that."

"Well I hope your brothers gone fuck you tonight since its always about them."

"You couldn't deny this dick if you want to. Look how it just sits on my thigh. Your mouth watering just looking at the tip. Go to bed Loosey, I'll wake you up when I get back."

"K daddy." Laughing, I headed downstairs, so we could go. Everybody was already down there waiting on me.

"G and Suave, why yall not dressed?" These niggas looked like earlier.

"Because I don't feel like dealing with your extra ass tonight. I'm going home to get in some pussy." Grabbing our keys, I got the extra set and handed it to Vic.

"What are these for?" He was looking confused.

"You can't do the brother line in that ugly ass Camry."

"It's a rental. My shit wet back home."

"Well you're here and you not doing the line with that car." I was glad Face agreed with me.

"What the fuck is the line?"

"You will see when you get there. Just do what you see us do." Walking out, we jumped in our

Phantoms. Vic was shocked his keys were to one as well. Heading to Hoover Nights, I could already feel the adrenaline. As soon as we rounded the corner, my ass went into Hollywood mode. Someone spotted us, and they started screaming. Once everyone realized what all the commotion was, they went crazy as well.

Pulling up in our line, we got in our spot one by one. You could tell the crowd was confused by the fifth car. We have never taken an extra car. If someone came with us, they rode in the car with one of the brothers. Since he was a brother, I felt it was only right for him to have his own. Clicking our lights off one by one, I looked back to make sure Vic had done it as well.

When he saw us open our door, he followed suit. You could see the excitement on his face. Stepping to the other side of our car, we let the crowd take us in. They started our chant, and it felt good to hear that shit.

"HOOVER. HOOVER. HOOVER." Before I could start egging them on, Vic pumped his arm up and down doing our shit. It's like he was a natural. Joining in with him, the crowd went crazy.

"That nigga like you for real. He loving this shit." Walking inside the club, our security guided us through. When the DJ saw us, he did his ritual.

"Aww shit, yall know what it is. The Hoover Gang in the mother fucking building. Everybody put your fucking hands in the air and salute some real niggas." Our song played, and this was the one thing I hated to let go.

"I think I'm big Meech, Larry Hoover. Whipping work, hallelujah. One nation under God, real niggas getting money from the fucking start." As soon as we got in the VIP section, Vic started in.

"This shit will have a nigga amped the fuck up. Yall do this shit all the time?"

"Only when we go out. I love this shit, but we barely do it anymore since we retired.

"I'm thinking I don't want to go back to Kentucky. Have yall ever thought about getting back in the game? I mean, is it an option?" Looking over at him, I thought about it.

"Maybe."

THE END....

OTHER BOOKS BY LATOYA NICOLE

NO WAY OUT 1-2

GANGSTA'S PARADISE 1-2

ADDICTED TO HIS PAIN

LOVE AND WAR 1-4

I GOTTA BE THE ONE YOU LOVE

CREEPING WITH THE ENEMY 1-2

THE RISE AND FALL OF A CRIME GOD 1-2

A CRAZY KIND OF LOVE

ON THE 12TH DAY OF CHRISTMAS MY SAVAGE GAVE TO ME

14 REASONS TO LOVE YOU

CPSIA information can be obtained
at www.ICGtesting.com
Printed in the USA
LVHW081306300819
629518LV00013B/343/P